# SUBJECTS WE LOVE TO HATE

Afolabi Onadipe

Copyrights © 2026

All Rights Reserved.

No part of this book may be reproduced or transmitted in any form or by any means, electronic or mechanical, including photocopying, recording, or by any information storage and retrieval system without the written permission of the author, except where permitted by law.

# Table of Contents

# Chapter 1:
# Idunnu's World

Idunnu woke up to the rhythmic sound of the bustling market down the street — the calls of vendors setting up their stalls, the rumble of wooden carts over the uneven road, and the faint chatter of neighbors beginning their day. It marked the start of yet another busy morning in her small Nigerian town.

She reached lazily for her alarm clock, the red numbers glowing **6:00 AM**. The sun had barely risen, casting a soft golden glow through her window, but the house was already alive with activity. It was a school day.

With a reluctant sigh, Idunnu pulled herself out of bed, stretching her arms and rubbing her eyes. Her room, though small, was her most comfortable place. Textbooks and notebooks were stacked neatly beside her bed, mixed with a few scattered art supplies. The window by her desk overlooked the garden, where bright flowers bloomed throughout the year, adding color to her mornings.

Her mother's voice carried through the house from the kitchen. "Idunnu, don't forget to clean your room before you leave! Your father is coming back from the office later."

Her mother was hardworking, and constantly juggling multiple tasks at once; cooking, organizing, and calling out reminders. Idunnu often admired how effortless she made it all look.

In the kitchen, her younger brother, Tunde, was already up and munching on bread with peanut butter. At eight years old, he had endless energy and a mischievous charm that could brighten any room. They argued over small things sometimes, but beneath it all their bond was strong.

The moment he saw her, his face lit up. "Idunnu! Did you see my new football?" he asked eagerly. "I can't wait for us to play later!"

Idunnu smiled at his excitement. "Not now, Tunde. I need to get ready for school."

As she dressed, she paused at the mirror. Her thick, dark hair was neatly tied in a ponytail, and her brown skin glowed under the morning sun. Sometimes she felt comfortable with how she looked; other days she wished she could do more with her appearance. But today her real worries were not about her looks — they were about the two subjects she struggled with the most; French and Fine Arts.

French felt like a puzzle with missing pieces. No matter how she practiced, the words twisted in her mouth, refusing to sound the way Madame Julie insisted they should. Every lesson left her feeling smaller, as though the language itself was mocking her.

Fine Arts wasn't any kinder. She loved creativity, but the strict techniques, the endless shading rules, and the cold precision expected in every line drained all the joy out of it. Mrs. Gathermoses' sharp critiques made her feel as if her ideas didn't matter, and every mistake became another reminder that the subject simply wasn't meant for her. The thought of facing those classes again made her stomach sink.

By 7:30 AM, she stepped out of the house with her school bag slung over one shoulder. Her mother was outside chatting with their neighbor, Mrs. Oluwole. The streets were active with vendors opening shops, vehicles passing by, and the steady hum of a town fully awake.

St. Michael's, her school, was a twenty-minute walk away, though the morning heat always made it feel longer. The school stood behind tall walls, shaded here and there by overgrown trees that had been there longer than most students.

Inside the gates, familiar sounds greeted her; the chatter of students, laughter echoing through the walkways, and the sharp whistle of a teacher trying to restore order. She exchanged quick greetings with classmates as she made her way to her usual spot under the large bamboo tree, where her closest friend, Sylvia, was waving her over.

"Idunnu, are you ready for the viva?" Sylvia teased dramatically. "Because Madame Julie will have our heads if we're not."

Idunnu groaned inwardly.

When the school bell rang, signaling the start of the first lesson, Idunnu gathered her things and walked into class. Her stomach tightened instantly. It was Result Day. The day that always felt heavier than any exam. She knew she had worked hard in her other subjects, but it never seemed to matter. Fine Arts and French stood like shadows over her shoulder, ready to pull her grades — and her confidence — down again. No matter how much effort she poured into them, those two subjects always found a way to remind her of her weaknesses. Even before she sat down, she could already feel the familiar knot of worry forming in her chest.

Throughout the lecture, her mind drifted back to Sylvia's morning joke. She wished she could enjoy moments like that more often; simple, carefree interactions without the weight of school.

Maybe then school wouldn't feel like a battlefield, where Fine Arts and French stood as her biggest enemies.

Later that evening, she sat across from her father at the dinner table as he examined her result sheet. Her heartbeat felt loud, thudding in her chest. Her father, Simon, was a quiet, disciplined man. She loved him deeply, but when it came to academics, they often clashed. He believed in excellence; she believed she was trying.

The results reflected her hard work: straight A's in Literature, Mathematics, English, and Social Studies. She had put in so much effort. But there it was; a single, painful **C** in Fine Arts, written in bold red ink.

Her father's expression did not soften. Instead, he frowned, the crease between his brows deepening as he read.

"You failed in Arts and French again, Idunnu," he said, his voice low and disappointed.

The word *failed* struck her harder than she expected. It felt sharp and unfair, cutting straight through all the effort she had put in. She blinked, stunned, her throat tightening.

How could one subject erase all the A's she had worked so tirelessly for?

"Dad, I tried," she burst out, the emotions she'd held in all day rising too fast to contain. "I tried so hard. That subject… that teacher… it's just too much." Her voice shook, frustration and defeat tangled together. "She wants us to be perfect. Every line, every shade, everything. And I can't do it the way she wants." She hadn't meant for her voice to sound sharp, and guilt rushed in as soon as the words escaped.

"Why do I have to listen to that woman's ranting for hours?" she continued, unable to stop herself from defending. "She doesn't even care that I don't understand. She just wants us to draw and paint like geniuses."

Her father stared at her for a moment, unmoving. "It's bad enough that you don't like the subject," he said calmly, "but must you dislike the teacher as well?"

Idunnu froze. His question caught her off guard. "I'm sorry, Dad," she muttered, her voice small. Guilt and frustration twisted inside her. "Fine Arts just doesn't make sense to me. It feels like I'm not allowed to have my own ideas…" She looked down. "Mrs. Gathermoses always makes it seem like you're either doing it her way or you're wrong."

He sighed, his tone softer now. "Idunnu, not every subject will be enjoyable. That is part of learning. But that doesn't mean you should give up. You can't let one subject — or one teacher — ruin everything. All subjects are important, whether you like them or not."

She wanted to argue, to explain how overwhelmed she felt… but she stayed silent. He wouldn't understand. "Don't worry, Dad," she finally said and managed a small smile. "I'll try harder next time. I'll make you proud."

His expression softened slightly. "I know you will, Idunnu. I believe in you."

# Chapter 2:
# Idunnu's World

The sun hung high above the school courtyard as students bustled through the gates, their voices blending into a lively morning hum. The air carried a mix of warm dust, fresh-cut grass, and the faint smell of akara frying from the food stalls just outside the walls. Uniforms swished, shoes scuffed against the concrete, and laughter rose and fell like waves. Prefects blew whistles, trying—and failing—to control the chaos.

Idunnu walked beside Sylvia, her school bag bouncing lightly on her shoulders as they weaved through clusters of students. Around them, the school buzzed with the restless energy of a new day: boys kicking an early-morning football, girls adjusting ribbons, teachers hurrying across the courtyard with stacks of papers. It was loud, messy, familiar—St. Michael's at its peak.

"I still don't understand why they make us study French," Sylvia complained, tucking a loose strand of her braids behind her ear. "When will I ever use it? I can barely speak English properly, and they want us conjugating verbs in French?"

Idunnu smirked. Like her, Sylvia despised French for very good reasons. Their shared suffering had become a pillar of their friendship.

"Maybe one day you'll visit Paris," Idunnu teased, "and thank Madame Julie for all her shouting."

Sylvia scoffed, folding her arms dramatically. "Paris? The only place I'm going is my mother's boutique. And trust me, no one needs 'bonjour' or 'merci' to buy Ankara."

The two girls burst into laughter as they made their way across the open schoolyard. Near the big palm tree, a familiar crowd waved them over. Tobi — the class comedian — and Emmy, the gentle, studious girl who always had an answer for everything, stood waiting

"Morning, ladies," Tobi chimed, sliding into the circle with a mischievous smile that made Idunnu instantly suspicious. "Did you guys hear about Unexpected?"

"Unexpected?" Idunnu wrinkled her nose, scanning their faces like she'd missed a meeting she was never invited to.

Tobi nodded, lowering her voice like the hallway had ears. "Rumor has it… she got caught."

The group gasped in unison—sharp, dramatic little inhales—while Idunnu stood there blinking, completely outside the moment. "Hey! Who's Unexpected? Tell me too!"

"You know," Tobi said, grinning wider, "the cleaner lady. The one who's always mopping around the corridors? Quiet. Mind-your-business energy."

Idunnu nodded slowly. She knew exactly who they meant: the woman who always smelled faintly of lemon disinfectant, who kept her head down, her uniform crisp, her scarf neatly pinned, her shoes spotless. Unexpected was always polite. Always composed. Always… proper.

"So," Tobi continued, practically vibrating with excitement, "Lisa showed us her TikTok."

Idunnu stared at them, still waiting for the part that mattered. "Okay, and? It's TikTok. That's not a crime. Everybody has social media. How can she be fired for that?"

Sylvia leaned in, eyes bright. "Because she posted videos in school. Our school. And they were so inappropriate."

Idunnu's brows shot up. "Inappropriate… how?"

Emmy let out a laugh that was half amusement, half disbelief. "Let's show her."

Before Idunnu could respond, Emmy was already unlocking her phone, her long nails tapping the screen with purpose. She angled it toward Idunnu like she was about to reveal a secret file.

"Look," Emmy whispered, scrolling. "This is her."

Idunnu leaned in—and froze.

The video opened with the unmistakable background of their school: the same corridor tiles, the same pale walls, and the same noticeboard everyone ignored. But the woman on the screen wasn't the quiet, neatly dressed cleaner Idunnu knew. The outfit was… barely an outfit. The movements were bold, suggestive— too confident, too exposed, too loud for a place that demanded silence and discipline. The captions were worse. The comments were worse than that.

Idunnu's hand flew to her mouth. "Oh my God."

Emmy swiped to another clip. Then another. Each one felt more shocking than the last, like the phone was pulling Idunnu deeper into something she didn't want to understand.

Idunnu stepped back, genuinely rattled. "No. No, I can't believe this."

Tobi's eyes gleamed. "Right?"

Idunnu shook her head, still staring at the screen like it might change if she blinked. "But… Unexpected was always so nice. She was always well-dressed. Well-behaved. She always greeted everyone properly. I would never have expected—"

She cut herself off, realizing how ridiculous that sounded. "Wait—how did she even get caught? Like… who found this?"

Sylvia exhaled like she'd been waiting for that question. "One of the students reported it."

Idunnu's eyes widened. "A student?"

Tobi nodded, delighted. "Apparently someone saw the videos, recognized the hallway, and took screenshots. Then they went straight to the principal."

Emmy added, "Not even anonymously. Like full confidence. 'Sir, I have something to show you.'"

Idunnu blinked, trying to picture it—some student standing in the principal's office, phone in hand, while the adults watched their school corridor turn into a TikTok set. "That's… insane."

"And it gets worse," Tobi said, leaning closer again, voice dropping into a whisper. "When they started checking, they found out she'd been posting there for years."

"For years?" Idunnu repeated, almost choking on the words.

Sylvia nodded. "Years. Different corners. Different classrooms. Sometimes even outside the staffroom door."

Emmy made a face. "Like she was using the school property as her personal studio. Unjustly. Without permission. Just… filming and posting.

Idunnu's stomach flipped. The idea that it had been happening at her school while teachers taught, students learned, and cleaners cleaned, felt unreal. "So she's been doing this in the school for years and nobody noticed?"

Tobi shrugged.

Idunnu stared at them, still stunned. "I can't believe it."

Sylvia nodded. "They said it's not just about the videos. It's about the misuse of the school's property. The reputation. Everything." She sighed. "Anyway, ready for another round of torture with Madame Julie?"

Sylvia groaned. "Don't remind me. I had a dream she locked us in the classroom until we pronounced every single verb perfectly."

"That's not a dream," Emmy said lightly. "That's just Thursday."

The group laughed together, but as the first bell rang, a tight knot formed in Idunnu's stomach. The sound of laughter around her suddenly felt distant, fading under the weight of her rising anxiety. She wished she could float through the day as easily as Tobi joked, or as boldly as Sylvia complained but she couldn't. She *wanted* to excel in every subject; she wanted to walk into class without fear. Yet French and Fine Arts always felt like locked doors she didn't have the key to.

And today, both subjects were waiting for her back-to-back. The thought alone made her shoulders sag, her confidence shrinking just a little more with each step toward the classroom.

Inside the classroom, chatter filled the air until the sharp click of heels silenced everything. Madame Julie entered with her usual elegance, her posture straight, her expression unreadable. She was tall, composed, and carried herself like someone who had lived in France her entire life. Her piercing eyes always made students sit a little straighter.

"Silence," she commanded, her voice cutting cleanly through the room. The class obeyed instantly. "Today," she continued, "we will practice the passé composé. Who can tell me how to form it?"

The room fell dead silent. Not a whisper. Not even a shuffle. Sylvia nudged Idunnu quickly. "Don't look up. If you make eye contact, she'll call you."

But it was too late.

"Mademoiselle Idunnu," Madame Julie said, locking eyes with her. "Enlighten us."

Idunnu's eyes widened the instant her name left the teacher's mouth. A sudden wave of heat shot through her body. Her palms went clammy, her heartbeat stumbling into a fast, panicked rhythm. All at once, every head in the room turned toward her.

She swallowed hard.

"Um… you use *avoir* or *être* with the past participle," she began slowly, praying her voice wouldn't crack. "And… umm, you match the subject if it's *être*, right?"

Madame Julie paused, raised one sharply defined eyebrow — then nodded.

"Correct. But try to answer with confidence next time. In French, hesitation is no better than an error."

A ripple of chuckles moved through the class. Not loud, but loud enough to sting. Idunnu's cheeks burned as she sank lower in her seat, wishing her chair would swallow her whole.

*Confidence?* She thought bitterly. *How am I supposed to be confident when I barely understand French? When every word feels like it's wrestling with my tongue?*

Sylvia leaned over with a crooked grin. "Nice save," she whispered. "Madame Julie almost ate you alive."

After the grueling French lesson, Idunnu's dread only grew. Next was Fine Arts — her personal nightmare. As she neared the art room, her stomach tightened again, almost painfully this time. The room itself *should* have been inspiring: high ceilings that let in soft daylight, wide windows overlooking the courtyard, and every wall lined with colorful student artwork that looked good enough to be in a gallery.

But to Idunnu, those masterpieces didn't inspire; they mocked her. Each perfectly shaded portrait and flawless landscape reminded her just how far behind she felt, how every attempt she made seemed to fall apart the moment her pencil touched paper.

She slid into her usual seat beside Sylvia. Sylvia immediately opened her sketchbook and began doodling effortlessly, drawing little shapes and characters like it was second nature. Meanwhile, Idunnu stared down at her own pristine, empty sheet; painfully white, painfully expectant. Blank, just like her mind every time she tried to draw. It sat there daring her to create something, anything, while all she could feel was the slow, creeping sense of failure settling in her chest.

Mrs. Gbadamosi, known to the students as Mrs. Gathermoses, stood at the front of the room. The nickname had stuck after a senior joked that she was like Moses, gathering unwilling "followers" and leading them into the "promised land" of artistic talent. Mrs. Gathermoses carried herself with an air of stern authority. Her sharp jawline and intense eyes made her seem intimidating, though her passion for art was undeniable.

"Good afternoon, class," she announced. "Today we will practice perspective drawing. A crucial skill for any serious artist. It demands discipline and attention to detail."

Idunnu quietly groaned.

Mrs. Gathermoses turned to the board, her chalk strokes fluid and confident. "Perspective," she explained, "is about seeing the world as it truly is, not as you imagine it. Your lines must converge at the vanishing point. Without that, your drawing lacks structure."

Sylvia leaned close and murmured, "She sounds like she's talking about life."

Idunnu snorted before quickly covering her mouth.

Soon, the room filled with the scratch of pencils. Idunnu stared at her blank paper again. She drew a hesitant line, then another, trying to mirror the example on the board.

Mrs. Gathermoses began her rounds. Idunnu's heartbeat quickened as the teacher approached. When she finally reached her table, she paused, studying the page. Idunnu's stomach churned.

"Not bad, Idunnu," she said, though her tone remained flat. She tapped the page lightly. "But your vanishing point needs adjusting. All your lines must meet precisely."

Idunnu nodded, her cheeks warm with embarrassment.

"At least she said 'not bad,'" Sylvia whispered. "That's basically a gold medal."

Idunnu managed a weak laugh, though frustration simmered beneath it.

When the final bell rang, students spilled back into the courtyard. Under the palm tree, they swapped snacks and stories.

"Mrs. Gathermoses is determined to turn us all into artists whether we like it or not," Sylvia muttered, biting into her biscuit.

Tobi grinned. "She's building an art army. First she gathers her 'Moseses,' then she conquers the world."

Everyone erupted in laughter, including Idunnu — a genuine laugh this time.

Later, when the sun dipped and the courtyard glowed in soft gold, Idunnu allowed herself a quiet moment. She didn't know how, and she didn't know when, but she felt a small spark inside her; a desire to face her struggles in French and Fine Arts. Not for her teachers. Not for her father. For herself.

If Mrs. Gathermoses could gather her own "Moseses," maybe Idunnu could learn to lead herself toward her own promised land of confidence.

# Chapter 3:
# The Academic Differences

Morning sunlight filtered gently through the curtains of Idunnu's modest Lagos home, painting soft golden lines across the breakfast table. She sat with a pencil in hand, carefully practicing her French vocabulary. Her notebook lay open beside a steaming cup of tea, each page filled with her determined attempts to improve.

Her father, Mr. Simon, leaned over her shoulder, adjusting his reading glasses as he inspected her work.

*"Comment ça va?"* he asked, his French accent slightly hesitant but proud.

*"Ça va bien, Papa,"* Idunnu replied with a confident smile.

He nodded approvingly. "Good. Very good. You must keep practicing. Languages are doors to the world." His eyes softened before he added, "And Fine Arts? Have you improved on that portrait of Mama?"

Idunnu hesitated, her eyes drifting toward her younger brother, Tunde, who was flipping through a comic book at the far end of the table.

"It's… coming along," she muttered. "I'm still working on the shading."

Her mother poked her head out of the kitchen, wooden spoon in hand. "She's doing well," she said, "but she spends too much time drawing what should be done in less time."

"Mama!" Idunnu protested, folding her arms. "Drawing is not my cup of tea. You agreed last week!"

Her father chuckled. "Your mother is right, but so are you. Balance is key, my dear. Now go and get ready for school. I'll drop you off today."

At school, the sun had just begun casting its glow over the sprawling compound of St. Michael's. The courtyard buzzed with chatter, uniforms rustling and shoes tapping against concrete. Above it all, the shrill whistle of Mr. Akinlade — the school's feared disciplinary master — pierced the morning air, calling students to assembly.

Multiple lines of neatly dressed pupils formed quickly, tension hanging over them like morning fog.

Idunnu stood among her classmates, nervously shifting in her polished shoes. Her heart thumped as she avoided eye contact with Mr. Akinlade, who stalked the rows like a lion surveying prey.

Assembly began with prayers and announcements, then slid predictably into warnings about lateness and noise-making.

"Today," Mr. Akinlade boomed, pacing with his cane, "we address latecomers and noisemakers. If your name is on this list, step forward now!"

Idunnu's stomach dropped. She already knew her name was there. Thanks to Tunde's last-minute morning chaos, she'd been late more than once. And if that wasn't enough, Ranti — the class captain — made it her personal mission to write down her name for *anything*. Ever since the day they argued about seating arrangements, Ranti had decided she was guilty by default.

"Ranti, bring the list," Mr. Akinlade ordered.

Ranti smirked and strutted forward with a crumpled sheet of paper, her eyes glinting with quiet satisfaction.

Idunnu glanced around instinctively for Sylvia — her backup in times like this — but Sylvia was home sick with a fever. A wave of dread washed over her. If she was here, at least Idunnu could share the guilt with her.

Names were called one by one, each student stepping forward to receive punishment. The swish of the cane slicing through the air made Idunnu wince every time.

"Idunnu Adebayo!" Mr. Akinlade's voice boomed.

A ripple of whispers cut through the rows; pity from some, curiosity from others.

With her head held high, Idunnu stepped forward despite the fear coiling in her chest.

"Ten strokes," he announced, flexing the long cane.

Students could usually share punishments with friends — Sylvia would have taken half — but today, Idunnu was alone.

"Sir, I didn't make noise!" she protested, her voice trembling.

"Liar," Ranti hissed from behind the lines, her grin spreading wider.

Idunnu's chest tightened. She wanted to scream the truth, to demand fairness, to insist on proof. She couldn't defend herself, even though she knew she was innocent. Unlike other education system, there were no CCTV cameras here — no recordings, no proof, nothing she could use to clear her name.

"Hands forward!" Mr. Akinlade barked.

With trembling fingers, Idunnu extended her hands. There was no point defending herself. It was her words against Ranti.

The first stroke stung sharply, but she refused to cry out. She clenched her jaw, determined not to give anyone the satisfaction. By the fifth stroke, tears spilled down her cheeks despite her effort to hold them back. Some students looked away in sympathy. Others whispered. A few seemed almost entertained.

Her palms throbbed painfully, each heartbeat sending a fresh wave of heat up her arms. She kept her eyes down, too embarrassed to meet anyone's gaze.

When assembly finally ended, students hurried toward their classes. Tobi caught up to her, his face filled with concern.

"Idunnu, are you okay?"

"I'm fine," she lied softly, hiding her swollen palms behind her back.

"Ranti is wicked," Tobi muttered. "Everyone knows you didn't do anything."

"It doesn't matter," Idunnu whispered. "Without proof, no one will ever believe me."

Tobi placed a gentle hand on her shoulder. "Still… the way you stood there, refusing to cry? That wasn't weakness. That was courage."

She managed a small, tired smile.

Later that day, Miss Alade's name was written neatly on the chalkboard as Idunnu entered her new classroom. Miss Alade herself stood tall at the front — elegant, composed, and far from timid despite her soft smile.

English Literature began with Chinua Achebe. The class was settling comfortably into the discussion when the door creaked loudly.

James — self-proclaimed king of the class — swaggered in. His tie was loose, his shirt partly tucked, and his confidence annoyingly intact.

"Ah, James," Miss Alade said without looking up. "How kind of you to join us. Take your seat quickly."

James ignored her and slumped into his chair, legs spread across the aisle. A few students stifled nervous laughter.

As Miss Alade continued teaching, James tapped his pen loudly and whispered exaggerated comments to the boy beside him until the whispers became full-blown chatter.

"James," Miss Alade snapped mid-sentence. "Am I interrupting your broadcast?"

The class giggled.

James leaned back with a smirk. "No, Miss. You go on. I'm just handling the entertainment."

The snickering grew louder.

Miss Alade set her chalk down and faced him completely.

"You listen here, little rascal," she said firmly. "I do not tolerate nonsense in my class. If you continue, I will send you out — and you will regret it."

James smirked wider. "Do you know who my dad is?"

A hush fell over the room. Idunnu's eyes widened at how James answered back with zero respect.

Without missing a beat, Miss Alade replied, dripping with sarcasm, "Go home and ask your mother who your father is. Do I look like your mother?"

The class exploded in laughter. Even those who feared James couldn't help themselves. Idunnu, despite having the worst day, smiled. She was proud of Miss Alade for not tolerating James.

James sputtered, face reddening. "You can't talk to me like that! My father—"

"—is not in this classroom," she cut in sharply. "I don't care if he is the president. I am the authority here. Sit quietly or leave."

James wilted under her stare and slunk back into his seat.

Later under the shade of the mango tree at lunch, Idunnu, Tobi, and their friend Clara sat with plates of rice and beans, replaying the dramatic classroom showdown.

"Did you see his face?" Clara gasped, mimicking James's proud stance. "'Do you know who my dad is?'" She threw her head back dramatically.

Tobi nearly choked laughing. "And Miss Alade's comeback — ah! Legendary."

"I've never seen James so quiet," Clara added. "Teachers usually avoid confronting him."

"Not Miss Alade," Tobi said. "She didn't even blink."

Idunnu poked her rice thoughtfully.

"You're quiet," Clara said gently. "What's on your mind?"

"It's not that I'm not impressed," Idunnu replied. "I just… keep wondering why James acts that way. Why he needs to be so entitled."

"Because he can," Tobi shrugged. "His parents spoil him. He feels untouchable."

Clara rolled her eyes. "He doesn't know what punishment is, I'm sure."

"It still isn't right," Idunnu murmured. "People shouldn't be allowed to make others feel small. It is not right."

Clara nodded. "Maybe Miss Alade will knock some sense into him."

"You think he'll change?" Idunnu asked skeptically.

"Not overnight," Tobi said, "but at least now he knows someone isn't afraid of him."

Idunnu sighed softly. "I just hope Miss Alade doesn't get in trouble with his father. You know how he gets."

Clara shrugged confidently. "She looks like the type who can handle anything."

A small smile tugged at Idunnu's lips. "She's exactly the kind of teacher this school needs."

The bell rang. Students began heading back toward the classrooms.

As Idunnu stood and dusted off her skirt, a quiet hope bloomed inside her — fragile, but real.

"Maybe this year will be different," she whispered as she walked beside her friends. Maybe she was stronger than she thought — stronger than the punishments, the unfairness, the difficult subjects, the loud classrooms.

With each step back toward the building, the weight on her chest lightened just a little, replaced by something she hadn't felt in a long time: the quiet belief that she could handle whatever came next.

# Chapter 4:
# The Odd Uncle Muniru

The family sat around the dinner table, the air warm with the smell of pepper, fried plantain, and stew. Plates clinked softly as everyone settled into eating. Tunde was already halfway through his food, chewing with the serious focus of someone who believed dinner was a competitive sport.

"So, how was school?" Mrs. Adebayo asked, scooping a small portion onto her spoon.

"It was fi—" Idunnu started automatically, then the image of Emmy's phone flashed in her mind. Her appetite paused for a second. "Actually… you remember that cleaner lady you gave water to the day you dropped me at school?"

Mrs. Adebayo looked up immediately. "Oh yes. She was young and looked like such a lovely girl." She shook her head with a small smile. "Very polite too."

Tunde perked up. "Cleaner lady?"

Mr. Simon frowned slightly. "The one near the corridor? What about her?"

"Well…" Idunnu sighed, pushing rice around her plate. "She was fired."

Tunde's eyes widened. "Fired like… pshhh?" He made a dramatic sound effect and waved his hand like someone being thrown out of a building.

"Tunde," Mrs. Adebayo warned, but even she looked unsettled. "Fired for what?"

Idunnu hesitated, then said it quickly, like ripping off plaster. "She was posting inappropriate videos on TikTok... inside the school."

"In the school?" Mrs. Adebayo's voice rose. "As in, on the school premises?"

Idunnu nodded. "Yes. Like... the actual corridors. Places we walk every day."

Mr. Simon's face hardened. "That is unacceptable. How did they even find out?"

"One student reported it to the principal," Idunnu said. "They recognized the background and took screenshots."

Tunde leaned forward, whispering loudly. "So the student snitched?"

Mrs. Adebayo turned to him sharply. "It is not snitching when someone is doing something wrong, Tunde. It is reporting."

Mr. Simon nodded once. "Good. That student did the right thing."

Idunnu looked up. "You're not angry that the student reported her?"

"Angry?" Mrs. Adebayo echoed, almost offended. "Why would I be angry? My daughter, that is exactly what students should do. If something is wrong in school, you report it to the right authority."

Mr. Simon pointed gently with his fork. "Not gossiping in corners. Not spreading it on group chats. You report it—properly."

Idunnu swallowed. "But everyone was talking about it today. Like it was entertainment."

Mrs. Adebayo sighed. "That is how trouble grows. People like to discuss problems, but they don't like to solve them."

Mr. Simon added, "And when people keep quiet, bad behavior continues. Imagine—years. It means nobody spoke up until now."

Idunnu nodded slowly. "I didn't even know what to think. She always looked so… normal. Nice. Well-dressed."

"That is why you must not judge only by appearance," Mrs. Adebayo said firmly. "A person can smile at you and still be doing something dangerous."

Idunnu shrugged. "I mean…don't you think she deserves a bit of pity, maybe? She did lose her job. And you know how we always said 'Unexpected,' is such a weird name? Well, Sylvia told me her parents named her that because her parents were not expecting her when the baby came…" She looked down. "The only acceptance and validation she ever got was from her 20,000 something followers, you know?"

Mrs. Adebayo smiled looking at her Idunnu as her daughter continued, "Imagine not even knowing how the feeling of love feels like until a stranger on internet tell you…"

Mr. Simon's voice stayed calm, but his eyes were serious. "Yes, I agree. That is unfortunate. That is why your mother and I always tell you kids to love yourself. Do not ever wait for other to acknowledge or validate you. You are enough the moment you were born."

Mrs. Adebayo reached across the table and touched Idunnu's hand. "And, if you ever see something that feels wrong—something unsafe, inappropriate, or suspicious—you tell your teacher or the principal. And you tell us too."

Idunnu looked down. "I didn't tell you immediately. I was going to just say 'fine.'"

"And that is why parents must ask," Mrs. Adebayo said gently. "If we don't ask, we won't know. If we don't know, we can't guide you."

Mr. Simon nodded. "From today, we're not accepting 'fine' again."

Tunde grinned. "So she has to talk every day now?"

"Yes," Mr. Simon said, looking at both of them. "Both of you."

Tunde's grin faded. "Ah."

Idunnu gave a small, reluctant smile. "So what should I say?"

Mrs. Adebayo smiled back. "You will tell us one good thing, one hard thing, and one thing you learned. Every day."

Tunde groaned dramatically. "That is three things!"

"And you will survive," Mrs. Adebayo replied, unimpressed.

Mr. Simon's tone softened. "This is how we keep you safe. You report what is wrong, and we stay involved enough to help you handle it."

Mrs. Adebayo squeezed Idunnu's hand once more. "So, my daughter... apart from Unexpected, what else happened today?"

Idunnu took a breath, and this time, she didn't say "fine."

Later, it was barely dawn when Idunnu's mother sat on the edge of the bed, arms crossed, lips pulled into a tight, worried line. The room was still dim, lit only by the soft golden glow of the bedside lamp. Her husband, Mr. Simon, lay sprawled across the mattress, half asleep with one arm thrown lazily over his forehead. She looked at him then looked away, finally, she gave in.

"Honey," she began, her tone low but edged with concern, "how much do you really know about this new driver of yours; Uncle Muniru? Something about him doesn't sit right with me. I can't trust him with the kids."

Mr. Simon groaned, rolling over with the exhaustion of someone who had heard this speech one too many times. "Not this again. Please. We've already talked about him."

"This is not something we should ignore," she snapped softly. "I have a very bad feeling about him. He behaves like a tout, and the kind of music he plays in the car is just... wrong for the kids. I told you this before, but you didn't take me seriously. If it were up to me, I would sack him already."

Mr. Simon sat up with visible reluctance, rubbing the sleep from his eyes. "You and Idunnu are the same," he muttered. "You just don't like him, so you brand him as bad. What has he done again?"

"For one, he shows no respect to anyone unless it's you," she retorted, her frustration rising. "And the constant swearing—do you want the children picking that up?"

Mr. Simon sighed deeply. "I'm busy, honey. That's the whole reason I hired him—to make things easier. Do you really want me leaving work just to pick up the kids? Firing him now is not an option."

She shook her head in exasperation. "Fine. But don't say I didn't warn you."

"Please," he muttered, flopping back onto the pillow. "Let's sleep. We'll talk about it tomorrow."

The following morning, Muniru rolled into the compound earlier than usual. His beat-up car didn't just arrive, it announced itself, rattling like loose metal in a blender. Before the doorman even finished sliding the gate open, the stereo exploded to life, blasting loud, thumping street music that shook the windows as if the house itself were protesting.

Idunnu's mother stormed to the window, the curtain swishing angrily in her hand. Her eyes widened with pure irritation.

"This man will drive me insane."

Outside, Mr. Simon was already dressed neatly for work, strode toward the car with the energy of a man trying very hard not to lose his patience.

"Muniru!" he barked. "Turn that down. You're disturbing everyone."

Muniru obeyed instantly, though the way he muttered under his breath made it clear he was only doing it because *Mr. Simon* said so. He treated everyone else in the house like background noise.

When Idunnu and Tunde finally rushed out, school bags bouncing behind them, Muniru flashed a wide, gap-toothed grin, a chewing stick dangling lazily from the corner of his mouth like it belonged there.

"Good morning, my kids!" he sang, voice too cheerful for the hour, and muffled by the stick.

"Good morning, Uncle Muniru," Tunde replied, already half-laughing, already too impressed.

Idunnu only gave a stiff nod.

Something about Muniru always felt… unsettling. The slang. The swearing. The careless disrespect he tossed at people like confetti. He wasn't dangerous — at least, not in a way she could name — but there was something in him that set every nerve in her body on alert.

So she stayed quiet. Silence was safer.

As soon as the car lurched out of the compound and bounced onto the main road, the performance began. As soon as the car lurched out of the compound and bounced onto the main road, Muniru transformed. His grip tightened on the steering wheel, as he muttered at every bump and passerby. The early morning traffic thickened around them with okadas weaving recklessly, street hawkers darting between cars, impatient drivers blaring horns as if it were a competition. Idunnu felt her shoulders tighten; she braced herself, knowing what came next. Muniru's eyes narrowed, his head leaned forward, and like a switch flipping

"Wèrè! Are you blind?" he roared at a pedestrian, leaning half out of the window.

A second later: "Ti e ma bá jé!" he snapped at a taxi swerving in front of him.

Idunnu flinched. Beside her, Tunde giggled, delighted. She elbowed him sharply. "Stop laughing. It's not funny."

But Tunde only covered his mouth, snickering harder as he whispered another insult, mimicking Muniru's tone perfectly.

Idunnu slumped back in her seat, turning her face toward the window. Cars whizzed by in a blur. The morning sun flashed between buildings. And all she could think was: If she could teleport out of this car and walk the entire distance to school, she absolutely would.

That evening, the family gathered in the living room where the soft glow of the television danced across the walls. Tunde sat cross-legged on the floor, completely absorbed in an episode of *Super Strikers*. Every few seconds, he chirped, clapped, or bounced as his favourite character dribbled across the screen.

Then—

A missed goal.

A dramatic gasp.

Tunde threw his hands up and shouted, **"Madman!"** with the same excitement someone else might shout *Goal!*

The room froze.

Their mother whipped around so fast her wrapper swished. Her eyes widened, sharp and stunned, as though she had just heard a fire alarm.

"What did you just say?" she demanded, marching toward him.

Still half lost in the cartoon, Tunde blinked up innocently. "Madman," he repeated with a proud little smile.

The remote disappeared from his hands in an instant. "Tunde! Where did you get that word? Where?"

He frowned, confused. "Uncle Muniru uses it all the time."

From the corner, their father lowered his newspaper with a long, weary sigh. "Darling, don't worry ab—"

"Don't worry?" she cut in, voice rising, hand flying to her hip. "Do you *understand* what just happened? Our son; your son just called someone a madman! An eight-year-old boy! Do you think that's normal?"

Their father sat back, frowning. "It's not ideal, I know, but it's hardly the end of the world. Children hear things everywhere. He probably doesn't even know what it means."

"Exactly!" she snapped. "He does *not* know what it means, which makes it worse! He's saying it like it's nothing!" She paced the room, each step hitting the tiles with sharp, angry precision.

Tunde shrank into the couch cushions, his smile fading, and his fingers fidgeting with the hem of his shirt.

"Look at him!" she exclaimed, pointing at Tunde. "Do you want him shouting insults at his classmates? Or teachers? Do you want him labelled as a disrespectful child? Because that's where this is heading if we ignore it."

Mr. Simon lifted his hands defensively. "Okay, okay. We'll talk to him. We'll explain it's not a good word. He's not running around cursing every day."

"You think it's that simple?" Her voice sharpened. "This isn't just about one word. It's about *exposure*. These children sit in the car with Uncle Muniru for almost two hours every day. Do you know what they're absorbing? The music. The language. The attitude. He is shaping them more than we are!"

Her words hung heavy in the air. The father shifted uncomfortably, guilt flickering across his expression.

She lowered her voice, but it was even more intense now. "The words they hear now… they carry them. What if Tunde repeats that in school? What if Idunnu starts talking like him? What kind of people are we raising if we let someone like Muniru be their example? Think about it."

Tunde looked up slowly, eyes wide and watery. "Mummy… sorry. I didn't know it was a bad word."

Her anger melted instantly. She knelt and gently cupped his face. "I know, sweetheart. I'm not angry at you. I'm upset because you didn't know. That's why we teach you. Do you understand why you shouldn't say things like that?"

He nodded timidly.

She rose again, her resolve stronger than before. "We need to decide, Simon. Either you set strict boundaries with Muniru, or we replace him. I'm serious. I won't let our children soak up behaviour they don't fully understand."

Her husband rubbed his temples, torn, but finally nodded. "Alright. I'll talk to him."

"Good," she said firmly. "Because this is about more than words. It's about who our children become."

Across the room, Idunnu watched quietly. A small part of her felt vindicated—her mother had sensed the danger from the start. But another part of her twisted with worry.

Muniru was a problem. Everyone could finally see that. But how far would things have to go before her father truly understood how serious it was?

And for the first time, she wondered if her mother's fear wasn't just worry, but a warning.

A warning they might have been too late to hear.

# Chapter 5:
# The Journey Continues

The clinking of cutlery and low morning chatter gave life to the breakfast table. Soft sunlight filtered through the curtains, spreading warm, golden streaks across the polished dining surface and the steaming plates of akara, toast, and eggs.

Tunde sat cross-legged on his chair, swinging his legs and reaching for another piece of akara with the enthusiasm of someone who had forgotten all warnings about table manners. Beside him, Idunnu sipped her tea quietly, her eyes drifting between her plate and her mother's tense, distant expression.

Sometimes, Idunnu wished she could be like Tunde. He lived lightly, fearlessly. He had already forgotten the chaos of the previous night, the shouting, the tension, the fear in their mother's eyes. For him, life reset every morning like a cartoon episode. Everything was new, funny, uncomplicated. But Idunnu felt everything.

She noticed the mood shifts in the house long before anyone said a word. She noticed the way her mother stirred her tea too slowly, the way her father was behind his newspaper, the way the air felt heavier than the sunlight tried to make it. While Tunde had already bounced back to his carefree self, Idunnu sat quietly, absorbing the discomfort filling the room like smoke.

Mrs. Adebayo sat at the head of the table, gazing fixedly upon her children, but her thoughts were elsewhere. Her usual warm brown eyes had a shadow of unease beneath them. She absent-mindedly stirred her tea, the spoon clinking against the porcelain cup. Her husband sat beside her with a newspaper spread open before him.

"Eat slowly, Tunde," Mrs. Adebayo said softly but sharply enough to make him pause.

She glanced at her husband, her lips pressing into a thin line. Mr. Simon hadn't noticed and the growing discomfort as Mrs. Adebayo attempted to concentrate on this pleasant morning scene, her mind going back to what she had heard from children: those unsettling encounters with Uncle Muniru. That man had a unique talent for inserting himself into their lives, but something bothered her skin. It wasn't just his pungent language or rude attitude; something was just off about him.

It wasn't just that the man was rude. Or careless. Or utterly lacking manners. It was something deeper. Something she couldn't name. Something that felt *wrong*.

Wrong enough to keep her awake last night.

Wrong enough to make her sit at the breakfast table with a heaviness that she couldn't shake.

And though no one had said his name yet, they were all thinking it; even Idunnu, who stared into her cup as if it held answers.

Mrs. Adebayo watched as Idunnu peeled the boiled egg, lifting each tiny shard of shell with the precision of a surgeon. The girl's brows were knit tightly, her lips pursed in a concentration far too serious for breakfast. Mrs. Adebayo sighed. Her daughter was carrying weight she shouldn't have to carry. And then, she decided to break the tension.

"Idunnu," she said, adopting a playful tone, "are you peeling that egg or interrogating it? At this rate, it might confess something before you eat it."

Tunde nearly choked on his akara. "Maybe the egg is hiding secrets!" he squealed, eyes wide with mischief. "Like where all the chickens are escaping to!"

Idunnu blinked in surprise, caught off guard by the attention. A tiny smile tugged at her lips before she managed to stifle it. "I just don't want to eat any bits of shell," she muttered, but the faint amusement in her eyes betrayed her.

Mrs. Adebayo spotted the opportunity to keep things light-hearted. She stretched out, plucked yet another boiled egg from the plate, and held it aloft dramatically. "This egg," she started in a whisper of conspiracy, "was the uprising leader in the chicken coup. They called her..." Chuck Norris".

Tunde burst out into uncontrolled laughter, pounding his fist on the table. "Chuck Norris! Mommy, that's brilliant!"

Even Idunnu couldn't hold back a chuckle. "Mummy, that is ridiculous," she said, shaking her head, but the tension in her shoulders seemed to ease as she finally bit into her carefully peeled egg.

"Well, you never know," Mrs. Adebayo, said with a shrug, her smile widening. "Chickens are smarter than we think. Why do you think they cross the road all the time? They are planning their next big escape."

Tunde was practically rolling with laughter now, and even Mr. Simon looked up from his newspaper with a bemused smile. Mrs. Adebayo leaned back in her chair, feeling a flicker of triumph. For a moment, at least, she had lifted the weight from her daughter's young shoulders and filled the room with laughter.

However, as she turned back to Idunnu, the fleeting shadow of worry passed over her face. Mrs. Adebayo's resolve deepened. The humor had helped, but it would not erase the unease. She would find a way to protect her children; she would not let it go.Not when her instincts screamed that keeping silent might cost her far more than she was willing to lose.

"Simon," her tone was strict. Her husband looked up from the paper, startled. "I'm worried about the children with Muniru. We need to do something about him."

Mr. Simon let his breath out slowly as he folded the paper. "Not this again," he muttered, though his tone was almost resigned. "Let them eat their breakfast in peace, darling. We'll talk later."

But Mrs. Adebayo couldn't let it go. Not when every instinct told her that leaving her children in that man's care was a mistake she could not afford to make. Before she could continue, Uncle Muniru's battered vehicle jolted forward, groaning as if it hated the road beneath it. The car bounced over a small pothole, the seats rattling, the windows vibrating in their frames. In the driver's seat, Muniru tapped his fingers against the steering wheel, humming loudly to whatever tune played in his head. His chewing stick bobbed between his teeth in steady rhythm.

Idunnu sighed, slung her school bag over her shoulder, and headed out the door with Tunde following closely behind.

"Have a great day at school!" Mrs. Adebayo called after them, but her voice held a thin strand of worry she couldn't hide.

The moment the kids settled into the backseat, Muniru reached into the front, grabbed a rumpled brown paper bag, and tossed it backward without looking. It landed between Idunnu and Tunde with a dull thump with its contents releasing a faint, unmistakable smell- it smelt of fried dough and roasting peanuts. Its tang filled the small car, blending with the smell of petrol and yesterday's rain, which hung in the air.

"Here, my children! Fresh snacks! I bought them just for you on the way," Uncle Muniru announced in a voice that boomed with joy as if he were narrating an advertisement. He threw them a glance from the rearview mirror and grinned to show his bright, complete teeth, his eyes crinkling in apparent delight.

Idunnu instantly uttered, "No, we just had breakfast, we're full. Thanks."

On the other side, Tunde's face lit up like a firework. "Thank you, Uncle Muniru!" he exclaimed, his hands darting forward to grasp the bag before it even settled. He tore it open eagerly, revealing golden puff-puffs, their crisp edges glistening with tiny oil droplets, and a handful of salted peanuts wrapped in thin cellophane.

The smell didn't comfort her.

It just reminded her how… off everything felt with him.

"Tunde, wait," she said quickly, her voice sharp and shaky.

But Tunde barely looked at her. He had already unwrapped a puff-puff and stuffed half of it into his mouth, grinning like he had found treasure.

"What?" he mumbled through the dough.

Idunnu clenched her fists so tightly her nails dug into her palms. "Don't eat it," she whispered urgently, sliding closer to him. Her eyes flicked up to the rear-view mirror where Uncle Muniru's teasing smile appeared between glances at the road. "Mum said we shouldn't take food from people we don't trust."

Tunde rolled his eyes and reached for another puff-puff. "Mum worries about everything," he said, shrugging. "It's just snacks. Uncle Muniru won't give us anything bad."

"You don't know that!" Idunnu hissed, her voice low but sharp. Fear and irritation simmered in her chest. "How do you know where it came from? What if—it's just not safe?"

Uncle Muniru chuckled loudly, the kind of laugh that made the hairs on the back of her neck rise.

"Ah-ah, what is all this?" he said, glancing back as if it were all a joke. "Idunnu, you are too serious. Relax! The snacks are clean. Fresh from the roadside vendor. I even tasted one myself — delicious!" He smacked his lips loudly, exaggerating the sound.

Tunde laughed along with him, powdered sugar already on his lips as he took another bite.

Idunnu's stomach twisted. *Why doesn't he ever listen?* Why did she always feel like the only one who noticed when something didn't feel right?

"Tunde," she tried again, softer this time, her voice cracking. "Please. Stop eating it."

But Tunde's face hardened. He swallowed and frowned at her, irritated. "You're always scared of everything," he said bluntly. "It's just food."

"That's not the point!" she snapped back. The words came out louder than she meant. The air in the car thickened instantly.

Uncle Muniru laughed again, shaking his head like he was watching a comedy show. "Children," he said, grinning. "Always fighting over nothing. Eat, Tunde! Enjoy yourself. Life is too short to worry like your sister."

Heat rushed to Idunnu's face. She turned toward the window, blinking hard to keep the tears back. Her reflection stared back at her; worried, angry, helpless. She wanted to grab the bag and throw it out of the car, shout at Tunde until he understood, but the fear of being wrong… or of making things worse… kept her quiet.

The car rattled on, filled with the sound of Tunde munching and Uncle Muniru humming loudly to the music.

Idunnu pressed her palm against her knee, her mind racing. She couldn't shake the feeling that something wasn't right; and that she was the only one who felt it.

A taxi swerved in front of them.

"Ti e ma bá jé!" Uncle Muniru shouted, leaning into the horn.

Tunde burst into giggles, whispering the insult under his breath like it was a line from his favorite cartoon.

"Tunde, don't," Idunnu said quietly, worn out. She wasn't angry anymore, just tired.

"So what? It's funny," he said, giving her a careless grin.

"It isn't funny," she said softly, her voice breaking as she stared out the window. "It's—"

But she couldn't finish. Her throat tightened, and she bit her lip hard as the tears finally filled her eyes. She turned her face toward the window and let them gather silently, hoping no one would notice.

And in that cramped, noisy car, Idunnu had never felt more alone.

# Chapter 6:
# The Troublesome Ride

Uncle Muniru was still humming off-key, completely unbothered by the fact that he sounded nothing like the music blaring from the speakers. The car rattled violently along the dirt track, every bump making the suspension grunt in protest. But Idunnu barely noticed any of it.

Her eyes were glued to Tunde.

A few minutes ago, he had been his usual self. Laughing, singing, copying Uncle Muniru's loud insults like he thought it was the funniest thing in the world. But now he sat slumped in his seat, his half-eaten packet of crisps dangling loosely from his fingers. His eyelids drooped heavily, his head tilting to the side like a sleepy toddler.

"Tunde?" Idunnu's voice cut sharply through the chaos. She leaned forward and shook his arm.

"Hm?" he mumbled, barely opening his eyes. His voice was thick, slow. "I'm… just tired, Idunnu. Let me sleep."

Idunnu's stomach twisted.

*Tunde? Tired? Now?*

That didn't make sense. Tunde never slept on the way to school. He was always the loudest person in the car, bouncing with energy, poking her arm, asking endless questions, humming cartoons, or reminding her how "boring" school was going to be.

But now—

"Tunde," she said again, her voice trembling as she shook him harder. "Wake up."

His head flopped back against the seat, his eyelids half-closed. There was a faint smile on his lips, but something about it made her chest tighten even more. His words came out soft, slow, like he was sinking into something he couldn't pull himself out of.

Her mind raced.

*Tunde doesn't nap. Not in the mornings. Not ever.*

Unless he was sick. Or exhausted. Or—

No. No, this wasn't normal.

Memories flashed through her mind; Tunde giggling earlier, imitating Uncle Muniru's shouting, the puff-puff, the snacks tossed carelessly into the backseat.

A cold wave washed through her.

Something was wrong. Very wrong.

And as the car rattled on, Idunnu's pulse hammered in her ears. She could feel it ; that prickling sense in her chest again. The one she felt whenever her instincts screamed louder than her thoughts.

"Tunde… please wake up," she whispered, fear creeping into her voice.

But he only slumped further, slipping deeper into the strange, heavy silence that didn't belong to him at all.

She shifted her gaze to the crumpled snack bag resting on Tunde's lap, her stomach tightening with a growing sense of dread. *Were the snacks the problem?* The thought lodged itself in her mind like a stone. She hadn't eaten any, not that it mattered much to Uncle Muniru, who never accepted hesitation and always insisted his food was "fresh, just for you." Tunde, being trusting and quick to believe anything that sounded exciting, had eaten without a second thought.

Her fingers curled into fists as she tried to steady her breathing, her mother's voice echoing sharply in her head:

*Always watch out for your brother, Idunnu. He's younger, and he doesn't think about the consequences.*

That reminder weighed heavily on her now, pressing down like a responsibility she hadn't been prepared for but suddenly had no choice but to carry.

She glanced at Uncle Muniru again. His humming, loud and off-key, grated against her nerves, and the grin he kept flashing into the rearview mirror made her stomach turn. Something felt wrong. Terribly wrong and Tunde's unusual quietness only deepened the knot forming in her chest.

Should she call her father? Should she confront Muniru directly? Her mind swirled with half-formed decisions, but underneath them all was a sickening, unspoken fear:

*What if it was already too late?*

She forced herself to speak.

"Uncle Muniru," she said, trying hard to keep her voice steady despite the tremor creeping in, "what was in those snacks?"

"Snacks?" he repeated, lifting his brow as though she were asking about something absurd. Then, with a wide grin that revealed his bright white teeth, he added, "Ah, my dear, nothing serious. Just snacks. Sweet treats for sweet children. Don't trouble your head, eh?"

Idunnu's heart sank. Her mother's warning rang even louder now:

*Never take food from strangers.*

She turned back to Tunde. He had slumped further into the seat, his breathing slow and far too steady for a child who was usually buzzing with life.

Her pulse hammered painfully as she reached into her school bag, her fingers fumbling blindly for her phone. She had to call her father. She needed him to know something wasn't right. And she needed him to know now.

"What are you doing?" Uncle Muniru's voice cut through her panic like a knife.

Idunnu ignored him, unlocking her phone with trembling hands. But before she could dial, Muniru parked by the roadside after yanking the phone from her hand.

"Hey!" she shouted, lunging forward, but Uncle Muniru was faster. He held the phone out of reach, his grin replaced with a dark, threatening expression.

"Aa-ah! What is this now?" Uncle Muniru snapped, his voice dropping into a low, dangerous rumble that made every hair on Idunnu's arms rise. "You do not trust your Uncle Muniru? Why will you now be suspicious of me, eh

"Give it back!" Idunnu cried, her voice cracking as the panic clawed up her throat. Her eyes stung, tears pricking fiercely, but she refused to let them fall. "Give it back! I will call my dad!"

"Ah-ah, you don't have to do all that," he said softly as though he were speaking to a toddler throwing a tantrum. But the calmness in his tone was betrayed by the cold glimmer in his eyes. "Relax, my dear. You are worrying yourself for nothing. You will only tire your small body."

Idunnu's pulse thundered in her ears as she watched him reach casually toward the glove compartment. One hand remained on the steering wheel, steady and practiced, while the other rifled through the mess inside until he pulled out a small bottle and a folded white cloth. The moment she saw them, her stomach dropped. Her mother's warnings, whispered in fear-laced tones, blurred through her mind. Every documentary her father ever watched suddenly replayed behind her eyes.

Her blood chilled.

She knew exactly what this was.

"No!" she screamed, her foot slamming into the back of his seat as hard as she could. "Leave me alone! Leave us alone!"

But he didn't even flinch. Without a word, he uncapped the bottle and poured the liquid onto the cloth. The sharp, chemical stench hit the air instantly; acrid, suffocating, unnatural.

Something inside Idunnu snapped.

She grabbed her schoolbag and swung it with every ounce of strength her trembling arms could muster. The bag struck the side of his head, scattering pencils, notebooks, and her water bottle across the seat and onto his shoulder. The car jerked violently, swerving as he shouted and momentarily lost control.

"That obstinate girl!" he roared, pounding the steering wheel as he regained balance.

The sudden movement jolted Tunde awake, if only slightly. His eyes fluttered open.

"Wh–what's… going on?" he mumbled, his voice soft and strangely limp, like he was speaking through a dream he couldn't fully wake from.

"Tunde, wake up! Please wake up!" Idunnu cried, choking on her tears as she fumbled desperately for the door handle.

"Sit down!" Muniru bellowed, swinging one arm back in an attempt to grab her.

But she twisted away, her small frame slipping right under his grasp. Her fingers found the lock, shaking violently, and she pushed the door open a few inches, the cold rush of air slapping her across the face.

"You'll hurt yourself, you foolish girl!" he barked, trying to steer with one hand and snatch at her with the other.

But Idunnu didn't care. She would rather tumble out of the moving car than stay trapped inside with him. With her heart hammering against her ribs, she sucked in a breath and let out a scream so raw, so piercing, it tore through the noise of the engine:

"HELP! Somebody help us! HELP!"

The car screeched violently to a stop. The sudden halt threw her forward, but she pushed off the seat and stumbled toward the open door. Muniru cursed loudly, scanning the surroundings with frantic eyes. They had stopped right beside a bustling roadside market; women frying puff-puff in oil, men loading crates, children running between stalls; all now turning toward the commotion.

Idunnu didn't hesitate. She threw the door wide open and leapt onto the dusty ground. She landed on her knees but she barely felt it. She scrambled to her feet and bolted toward the crowd, her voice cracking as she screamed for help.

Behind her, she heard Muniru shouting, his tone panicked, deceitful, desperate. "It's nothing o! Just children misbehaving! Nothing is happening!"

But the crowd wasn't buying it. Stall owners stepped forward, forming a barrier draped in aprons, wrappers, and sweat-soaked shirts, their expressions shifting from curiosity to suspicion to protective outrage.

Idunnu whipped around toward the car, pointing frantically. "Tunde! He's still inside! Please! Someone help him!"

But no one moved fast enough, not for her. Her chest tightened as helplessness clawed at her ribs. She couldn't leave her brother; she wouldn't. Panic churned through her thoughts, messy and fast;

*What if he took off again? What if he hurt Tunde? What if—*

Suddenly, a heavy hand clamped down on her shoulder.

She froze. Slowly, she turned.

It was him.

Uncle Muniru towered behind her, his face set into a cold, deadly stillness she had never seen before. "That is enough," he whispered; quiet, but suffocating, his voice coated in venom.

In his other hand was the white handkerchief. The moment it lifted toward her, the sharp, chemical smell flooded her senses.

"No—NO!" she cried, twisting, thrashing, her arms flailing wildly.

But his grip was iron.

Her vision blurred.

Her legs buckled.

Her mind flashed; her mother's voice, her father's laughter, Tunde's smile—

And then she remembered. Something she had once overheard her father say while watching a survival show.

*Sometimes, when you cannot fight back... you pretend.*

With the last flicker of consciousness, she let her body go slack.

Muniru hesitated, his brows furrowed as he studied her limp form. After a moment, satisfied, he grunted in approval. "Stupid girl," he muttered, dragging her like a rag doll back toward the waiting car.

Her heart hammered painfully inside her chest, but she did not move. She barely breathed. Pretending to sleep was her only shield—fragile, risky, desperate, but it was all she had.

The car jerked forward again, the engine growling as they pulled away from the market.

And though she kept her eyes closed, tears seeped out and ran down her temples, curling into her hairline.

*How did I let this happen?*

*Why didn't I stop him from eating those snacks?*

*Tunde is always so trusting, so carefree… why wasn't I stronger? Why didn't I try harder?*

Guilt crushed her chest, sharp and merciless. She wanted to scream, to fight, to rewind the morning and throw those snacks out of the window. But she could do nothing now—nothing except hold onto the faint, trembling hope that somehow, some way, she would get another chance.

Because beneath the fear, something else stirred; small, furious, burning like a spark.

Rage.

Rage at Muniru. Rage at his lies. Rage at his smile. Rage at how he had called them "his children" while planning something monstrous.

Her nails dug deep into her palms as she fought to stay conscious.

This wasn't over.

Not by far.

If anything, for Idunnu, this became a war.

# Chapter 7:
# Shadows in the Dark

Idunnu woke up to a dim, silent car. A soft murmur seeped through the walls. She could hear the quick, urgent words spoken in hushed tones. The language shifted to French, and though she understood only parts of it, she listened intently. Every moment since her abduction had etched itself into her memory like a scar, and tonight was no different.

The car remained still except for the faint hum of conversation nearby. She recognized one of the voices instantly; Uncle Muniru's. Low, rough, and commanding, it carried through the thin walls. He was speaking in French, a language Idunnu had learned to understand thanks to her mother's insistence that she grow familiar with it. She tilted her head slightly, focusing, determined to catch every word.

"…la vertu." Muniru said. "We need to switch before dawn. And, the car—we have to change it before first light."

A low murmur of agreement followed, then another voice; lighter, but edged with worry. "Et le point de rencontre? C'est toujours Igbo-Ora?"

*And the meeting point? Is it still Igbo-Ora?* Idunnu's mind instantly translated.

Muniru's tone sharpened. "Non, ça a changé. Maintenant, c'est à Ibarapa. Nous ne pouvons pas prendre de risques inutiles."

*No, it's changed. It's in Ibarapa now. We can't take unnecessary risks.*

Idunnu's heart hammered against her ribs. A vehicle switch meant they were hiding their trail. A new meeting point meant the plan was still moving—shifting, tightening—growing more dangerous with every passing minute. She lay completely still, unable to move even an inch; fear held her muscles rigid, locking her in place like stone.

A third voice joined in, carrying a tremor of anxiety. "Et la fille? Elle sait trop de choses."

*And the girl? She knows too much.*

"Elle est inutile sans son père," Muniru snapped.

*She's useless without her father.*

Idunnu gulped. The weight of his words settled over her like a suffocating blanket. *After, we'll see.* The phrase echoed in her mind, sharp as broken glass. What did that mean? Would they kill her once they no longer needed her? The thought struck her so hard she felt her stomach twist painfully.

She bit the inside of her cheek to stop herself from trembling. Her tongue tasted of iron, the bitterness grounding her just enough to stay silent. Every fibre of her being screamed at her to run, to escape—her legs twitched with the instinct—but she knew she couldn't. Not yet. One wrong breath, one wrong rustle, and they might remember she was awake.

The conversation shifted. The men's voices dropped to a low rumble, discussing logistics; routes, names she didn't know, clipped instructions she strained her ears to catch. Idunnu forced her brain to stay sharp despite the fear fogging her thoughts. She held onto every detail, no matter how small. These scraps of information were her only weapon, the only thread tying her to the possibility of survival.

Her pulse hammered so loudly she worried they might hear it.

*Switch cars before dawn. New meeting point in Ibarapa.*

In the car, as Idunnu heard the word *Sabo*, her heart jolted.

"Mokola Roundabout… Sabo… We need to exchange some money. I stole it from her father's car." Muniru's barked a laugh.

These were familiar places. Her grandfather—Baba Sabo, as everyone fondly called him—had been a respected businessman who owned several hotels in Ibadan. He spoke Hausa fluently and lived in Sabo for years, earning the nickname WAGADUGU. His mansion still stood there, a reminder of the legacy he left behind. Idunnu had grown up listening to stories about how her grandfather helped countless people. To many, he wasn't just a man—he was a protector. A legend.

Suddenly, a thought lit up inside her. This could be her chance. If the kidnappers stopped in Sabo, she might be able to draw attention—maybe even help herself and her brother escape. She whispered a silent prayer and held onto one thought with all her strength. And she hoped—hoped with every part of her—that the name her grandfather carried would still open hearts, and maybe, open a way out.

Her mind spun with possibilities; dangerous, fragile possibilities. If they changed vehicles before dawn, maybe there would be chaos… movement… a momentary lapse in attention. She could slip away, leave a clue, scream, fight—*something*. But she would have to be careful. Terrifyingly careful. A single misstep could cost her everything.

Their footsteps moved away, fading into the forest, the murmur of their voices swallowed by the car's door. Idunnu didn't dare move. She counted slowly to one hundred, her breaths tight and uneven, as though her lungs had forgotten how to work.

Only then did she open her eyes.

The car remained dark and empty except for the thin ribbon of moonlight leaking through the cracked window. Dust drifted lazily in the air, each speck catching the faint silver glow. She hadn't noticed the smell before—mildew, damp cloth, old leather—but now it wrapped around her nauseatingly.

She let herself breathe—really breathe—for the first time. But each inhale trembled. Each exhale felt like she was letting go of something she needed to hold onto.

She replayed the men's conversation in her mind, forcing the words to stick, carving them deep enough that panic couldn't wash them away.

Switch vehicles before dawn.

*Meeting point in Ibarapa.*

Her fate still undecided.

She sat up slowly, every movement deliberate, terrified that even the creak of the car's frame might betray her. Her mind was awake; stinging, alert, frantic. Somewhere out there, she knew her father was searching for her. She clung to that thought like a rope. She had to believe it. She had to stay alive for him, for her brother, for herself.

Finally, she lay back down, her body shuddering as the fear pressed in on her again. She closed her eyes, pretending sleep, but her mind refused to rest. She planned. She prayed. She waited for dawn as if it were a narrow doorway she needed to slip through before it slammed shut.

She had spent years rolling her eyes at French and Fine Arts. She never liked the subjects, never liked the teachers, and never saw the point of any of it. To her, they were useless — distractions from the subjects that truly mattered: Maths, English, the things that made sense and would "take her somewhere." She always believed those other classes were a waste of her time, a burden forced on her by adults who "didn't understand her future."

But in this terrifying moment, the very things she had dismissed were the ones reaching back to save her.

Her fluency in French — the same language she used to dread studying — suddenly became her lifeline. Had she not understood their whispered words, she would have been blind to the danger closing around her. But she *did* understand. She caught every warning, every threat, every piece of the puzzle they never meant for her to hear. And because she understood, she had a chance.

A chance for her brother.

A chance for herself.

A chance to survive.

And it was then she realized something she had never understood before: No subject is truly useless. Everything we learn, one day, finds its purpose.

.

# Chapter 8:
# Identity Reveal

**Idunnu didn't know how long she had been lying still.** Minutes? Hours? The darkness made time twist strangely. Her limbs were stiff, her neck ached from the awkward angle, and the cold mat beneath her pressed through her skin like stone.

She stared into the gloom, barely blinking. A part of her feared that even the slightest movement might draw someone's attention. The car had fallen silent again, but silence in this place didn't feel safe. It felt watchful. Her fingers curled instinctively into fists, the rough fabric of her dress scratching against her palms. She didn't even notice at first. Her whole body felt too tight, too small to hold the fear coiling inside her. Then— unexpectedly—her fine art teacher's voice rose in her mind, soft and steady, a memory surfacing like a hand reaching out to her.

"Observe the lines. The contours. A face tells a story."

For a moment, she imagined the classroom; the chalk tapping against the board, the tired ceiling fan rattling above them, the patient smile her teacher wore when explaining something for the tenth time. Idunnu squeezed her eyes shut, almost able to smell the chalk dust, almost able to hear the low hum of students' pencils scratching against paper.

"Even the slightest curve of a lip," her teacher would say, "or the depth of a furrow; everything reveals something. Learn to see beyond what is obvious."

She opened her eyes slowly. The memory steadied her.

Her gaze shifted back to the dark car, to the shadows stretching along the interior like crooked fingers. Her heart thudded hard, but her mind began to anchor itself around one thing she could control—observation.

Fragments of her captors' faces rose in her thoughts, sharper now. Muniru's angular jaw. The way his brow knotted when he gave orders. The nervous man's darting eyes and how his lips quivered when he spoke, like his courage was thinner than the air he breathed. And the third man; the one with the gaunt cheeks and deep grooves etched from nose to mouth, creases not just of age but of resignation.

Idunnu began sketching them in her mind.

A broad nose. Heavy stubble. The jagged scar slashing across Muniru's left temple.

She layered each detail carefully, the way she had been taught; shading, refining, and stepping back in her mind to see the whole face. If her life depended on remembering them—and it did—she would not forget a single line. Her teacher's voice drifted to her again:

"Faces are like maps. They tell where people have been. Sometimes, they hint at where they are going."

A shiver ran through her, not from the cold. She finally understood the power of paying attention. Her eyes moved slowly toward the door. One of the men stood outside, his shadow cast long across the floor. She watched his gait: the slight drag of his right foot, the way his body leaned forward as though bracing against a weight no one else could see. She stored it—all of it. These details were more than observations.

They were tools. They were weapons. They were her way out.

"Don't just see. Understand." Her teacher had said that once. Idunnu breathed it in now as if it were medicine.

Why did Muniru look so hardened? Why did the nervous one twitch like he feared the shadows themselves? Why did the third man hold himself like someone fulfilling a debt rather than a desire? Idunnu's pulse quickened as patterns formed. They weren't just captors; they were men with fears, tempers, and weaknesses. And she was beginning to see them.

Her fists slowly loosened as her thoughts sharpened. If she couldn't fight them with strength, she would fight with observation; with understanding.

A face tells a story, her teacher had taught her. And Idunnu was determined that, somehow, their faces would become part of *hers*: the story of a girl who refused to break. She ran through their features again. Muniru's strong jaw. The nervous man's furtive gaze. The third man's thin, pinched lips. Each detail steadying her, grounding her.

The men's voices drifted closer again, the hum of their conversation swelling as they returned to the car. Their words were rushed; a mix of French and local dialects. She leaned in, listening.

*Switch before dawn.*

*Ibarapa.*

*Keep the girl—for now.*

Their phrases weighed heavily, but they didn't paralyze her. Not anymore. They prepared her. The engine sputtered, gave a final shudder, and died. The car doors creaked open. One by one, the men stepped out, their boots crunching against gravel.

Idunnu inhaled deeply; slow, steady, deliberate.

She would remember. She would use everything. She would survive.

"She's asleep." One of them muttered.

"Good. Less trouble that way," Muniru replied coldly. "Let's move quickly."

The car doors slammed shut, and the kidnappers' voices faded as they walked away, their silhouettes swallowed by the night. Silence settled over the vehicle; deep, heavy, broken only by the restless chirping of crickets and the soft rustle of wind threading through the trees.

Idunnu's heart hammered against her ribs as she slowly opened her eyes. The car was engulfed in shadows, lit only by a thin wash of moonlight leaking in through the cracked window. She strained to hear any indication the men were returning. When none came, she released a shallow, shaky breath.

This was her chance. But the thought of Tunde rooted her in place.

The memory of their separation hit her like a punch. She could still hear his voice—frightened yet trying so hard to be brave—calling as the men dragged him into another car.

"Idunnu! Don't be scared!"

She had clung to his voice then. Now it felt like a wound. Tears pooled in her eyes, and she pressed a trembling hand over her mouth to stifle the sob rising in her throat.

*Where is he? Are they hurting him? Is he even alive?*

Each question burrowed deeper, each one worse than the last. She clenched her fists hard enough that her nails dug crescents into her palms. She knew panicking wouldn't save either of them. She pushed herself upright, moving with deliberate care. Her body felt stiff, her limbs heavy, but she forced her shaking hands to scan the car for anything—anything—that could help her.

The kidnappers had stripped her of almost everything.

But then she remembered Muniru snatching her phone and shoving it somewhere with a smirk. Her eyes darted to the dashboard. Holding her breath, she leaned forward, fingers brushing along the inner rim. Something crinkled—paper—and beneath it, the familiar edge of her small battered phone.

Her pulse surged.

She gripped it slowly, easing it free inch by inch so it wouldn't make a sound. When it finally slipped into her hand, she nearly cried out in relief.

She froze again, listening.

Nothing. Only the forest whispering outside.

She curled over the phone protectively, as though it were the last fragile thing keeping her alive. With a silent prayer, she pressed the power button. A faint glow lit her face. The screen flickered, dim but alive. A wave of relief washed through her so strong it made her dizzy.

She dialed her father's number with trembling fingers.

It rang once. Twice.

Then—

"Idunnu?"

His voice cracked on her name.

"It's me, Papa," she whispered, her voice shaking. "I… I don't have much time. They left the car. They said they're switching vehicles before dawn. The new meeting place is Ibarapa. Papa, please… come quickly."

Her father's breathing steadied, shifting into the calm, firm tone she had grown up trusting.

"Listen to me, Idunnu," he said. "Stay where you are. Stay quiet. I'm coming for you."

The line clicked.

Idunnu held the phone to her chest, her tears finally spilling; silent, messy, and unstoppable. Relief mingled with terror, but this time, she wasn't drowning in it. She had done something. She had acted. Sitting in the darkness of the abandoned car, Idunnu knew her ordeal wasn't over. But she had carved a small crack in the fear that surrounded her; a tiny act of courage in the middle of a nightmare.

Whatever happened next, she would face it.

For herself.

For Tunde.

And for the promise she made the moment she heard her father's voice:

*She would survive.*

# Chapter 9:
# Rescuing Idunnu

Idunnu laid still as the sound of leaves rustled outside. Her fingers clenched around the phone pressed to her chest, its edges digging into her palm. She didn't dare breathe. The last thing she wanted was to be caught with it.

She squeezed her eyes shut; so tight that tears slipped out despite her efforts. Suddenly, the phone rang. Her heartbeat hammered against her ribs as she quickly picked the phone and placed near her ear.

Silence.

"Idunnu?"

Her breath escaped her in a broken rush. She knew that voice. "Father?" she whispered, barely able to form the word.

Tears poured freely down her face as Idunnu, still shaken but resolute, told what she overheard in the few minutes she spent with the kidnappers—the car switch and the new meeting point spilling out of her in a rush of fear and determination.

"They spoke in French," Idunnu whispered in her call, her voice shaking but clear. "I didn't understand most of it, but a few phrases here and there. They mentioned 'rançon,' which means ransom. So, I was aware their target was to kidnap us for ransom. I also caught phrases about leaving the car before dawn and a location they called Ibarapa."

Mr. Simon was feeling the intensity of the situation with a tight jaw and his body stiff with unexpressed rage. His wife, Mrs. Adebayo, stood alongside him, clutching onto his arm as if finding support in his resolve. The police officer in charge, Inspector Kolade, nodded grimly with no expression.

"We need to move fast," Inspector Kolade said, addressing his team. "They should still be on the road. If we wait until tomorrow, they'll disappear once again."

Mr. Simon's voice was sharp, urgent. "You must find her before dawn. My daughter is strong, but she is just a child. Please, Inspector."

The inspector raised a reassuring hand. "We'll do everything we can. The details Miss Idunnu provided give us a starting point. Let's move out."

Meanwhile, in the dim darkness of the abandoned car, Idunnu clutched the phone, whose weak glow cast an eerie light upon her face. Her father's voice still echoed in her mind, grounding her amidst the chaos. She had done what she could. Now, she needed to stay alert and wait for her opportunity.

"Idunnu, listen to me. Stay put. Do not worry. We're coming to save you, okay?" Mr. Simon talked to her daughter.

Idunnu nodded, "Okay." She managed to mutter before the line went silent.

Her captors had not yet returned, and the silence surrounding her was at once both her relief and torment. When the car creaked, or leaves rustled outside, she knew her heart would jump like a jackrabbit in her chest. She had no notion of the time since these men left. For hours, it was just minutes.

Then, faint voices broke the quiet. The kidnappers were coming back. She quickly powered off the phone, slipping it into the waistband of her skirt. Flattening herself against the seat, she willed her breathing to slow as the car door creaked open.

"Get in," Muniru's gravelly voice ordered, his tone clipped and impatient.

The nervous man from earlier hesitated. "Should we leave her here? It's risky to keep moving with her."

Muniru's glare was almost tangible in the darkness. "She stays. For now. We're not leaving any loose ends. Now get in and shut up."

The men piled into the car, their movements hurried. The engine roared to life, and the vehicle lurched forward. Idunnu remained silent, her mind racing. If they were switching vehicles, they would have to stop again soon. That might be her chance to escape.

On the forest road, the search party moved at a brisk pace. The police convoy split into two groups; one proceeded toward Ibarapa, and the other tracked any sign of the kidnappers' route. Mr. Simon rode with Inspector Kolade, his eyes scanning the darkness outside him. Every fiber of his being was set on finding his daughter.

Mrs. Adebayo stayed at base camp, her hands clasped in prayer. Mr. Simon stayed with her, trying to comfort her. "She's smart," he whispered. "She'll figure out a way to live."

His wife shook her head in defeat, "My instincts were not wrong." She whispered as the room fell silent. "I knew Muniru was not clean since day one," she look at Mr. Simon, "But you wouldn't listen to me. Even when Idunnus said she wasn't comfortable with him…" Tears fell down her face. "You should've llistened to us, Simon." She whispered, 'You should have."

The kidnappers took a turn, drawing near a secluded clearing with dawn breaking. Another car— a battered pickup truck— was already there, awaiting them. Muniru went out first, his authoritative demeanour drawing the others after him.

"Fast," he growled. "Move everything over. We can't spend too much time."

Idunnu's heart raced. It was time. Her hour. She waited until the men became absorbed in unloading the car, their concentration centred on bags and crates coming out of the trunk. In complete silence, she skimmed across the seat as a shadow slid across a wall. Her fingers closed on the door handle and opened it, just the softest creak of metal breaking the silence.

"What was that?" The nervous man asked, his head snapping toward the car.

Idunnu froze, her breath caught in her throat. Muniru's eyes narrowed, scanning the area. "Probably an animal," he muttered. "Focus on the job."

As the men returned to their task, Idunnu quietly got out of the car and into the thicket. The cool night breeze bit at her cheeks as she walked, low to the ground, and kept herself hidden from view. Her bare feet felt against the soft earth with each deliberate, silent step.

Her heart pounded in her chest as she darted deeper into the forest. Behind her, the kidnappers' voices grew fainter, but she didn't stop. She couldn't risk it.

As the forest began to thin, Idunnu stumbled onto a narrow path, her breath ragged but her resolve unbroken. Behind her, the chaos of the night lingered like a fading echo. Miles away, meanwhile, the search party's focus sharpened with new clues, and the officer's voice over the radio reignited hope. "We've found tracks near a clearing off the main road," came the voice of an officer. "Looks like a second vehicle was here recently." It was a signal that could bring them closer to revealing the kidnappers' next move.

Mr. Simon leaned forward, urgency in his voice. "Was my daughter with them?"

"It's hard to say, sir. But some footprints go into the forest. Little ones."

A spark of hope lit up in his chest. "That's her. It has to be."

Inspector Kolade nodded. "We will follow the trail. Everyone, stay alert. They could still be near."

Idunnu limped through the woods, her legs on fire and her breath rasping. But she did not give up. A glimpse of the noise of voices coming up from her back propelled her. Just then, a beam of light appeared from between the trees before her and froze her.

"Idunnu!" her father's voice thundered strongly.

She raised her foot, wiping at her streaming eyes with a gesture. "Papa!"

In an instant, Mr. Simon emerged from the trees, his arms outstretched. Idunnu ran to him, collapsing into his embrace. Relief and gratitude washed over her as she clung to him, safe at last.

Before she could fully sit up, her father was already pulling her into his arms. The phone slipped from her fingers as her body folded into his, every muscle unravelling all at once. She felt herself melt against him, the tension of the night draining out of her in a single, shuddering breath. His embrace was tight—desperate—as though he feared she might vanish if he loosened his grip even for a heartbeat.

"Papa…" she whispered, the word breaking apart as it left her lips.

Tears poured freely down her face, soaking into the fabric of his shirt. Her father's hands trembled as he cradled the back of her head, murmuring her name over and over like a prayer finally answered.

"You're safe now, my baby. You're safe," he whispered, voice thick with relief and exhaustion.

For the first time since the nightmare began, Idunnu allowed herself to believe it. She clung to him, letting the warmth of his arms dissolve the cold fear that had lived in her chest all night. The forest around them seemed to exhale too—quiet, soft, no longer the enemy it had felt like moments ago.

But beneath the relief, one thought burned steady in her mind.

*Tunde.*

# Chapter 10: Post-Escape

The forest lay in stunned silence as dawn crept across the sky, brushing it with hues of gold and lavender. Idunnu, cradled tightly in her father's arms, allowed herself a single, trembling breath. She was safe — for now. But her mind refused to settle. Every detail from the harrowing night replayed in her mind like an unfinished sketch begging for completion.

Her brother's name pulsed through her thoughts like a steady drumbeat. He was still out there, still in their captors' hands. The thought made her chest tighten, fear and guilt twisting inside her. How could she feel even a flicker of relief when he was still missing?

His face flashed behind her eyelids; the mischievous grin, the light in his eyes, the way he always cracked a joke just to ease her nerves. She remembered his whispered words in the cramped car:

"Stay strong, Idunnu. We'll get through this."

But she was here, and he wasn't.

The weight of that truth burned through her like fire. She clenched her fists, anger bubbling beneath her skin. She had to help him. She wouldn't let the kidnappers win. Her parents guided her back to the base camp, where medics hurried forward. Mrs. Adebayo pulled Idunnu into a fierce embrace, tears streaming down her cheeks.

"My brave girl," she whispered, stroking her hair. "You're home now. You're safe."

Idunnu nodded, though her throat tightened. Safe was a luxury she couldn't accept yet. Work still remained. Tunde's voice echoed in her mind again: "You're the wise one, Idunnu — brains over brawn, always."

And she would prove him right.

As soon as she sat down, Inspector Kolade approached, pen and pad in hand. "Miss Idunnu, I know this is difficult," he began, "but anything you can recall may help us track these men down."

Her mind snapped to the present. The pressure of everything pressed on her chest like a hot iron. She curled her fists, nails digging into her palms; grounding her. Her resolve hardened, solidifying like metal forged in flame. There was no room for hesitation. No space for fear. Tunde needed her.

She inhaled deeply, pushing her panic aside and locking it away for later. If *later* even existed.

Her gaze met the inspector's. "I'll tell you everything I can," she said, voice steady despite the storm inside her.

Her heart thudded violently, but on the outside, she was calm. She had to be.

Her parents gave her a reassuring nod. Idunnu exhaled slowly. "I heard them talking in French. But I could understand most of what they were saying…" she began.

"You could?" Her mother looked at her wide-eyed.

Idunnu slyly smiled at her mother as the Inspector gave her an assured nod, "They said something about leaving the car before dawn and meeting at Ibarapa. One of them kept repeating the word *camion*… doesn't that mean 'truck'?"

Inspector Kolade nodded. "Yes. That's a very important detail. Go on."

Idunnu tightened her grip on the blanket someone had wrapped around her shoulders. She fought to piece together every scrap of conversation. "One of them was called Muniru," she said. "He was our driver and used to drive my brother and me to school. Through their conversations that I overheard, I came to realize he's actually the leader. Also, because the others seemed afraid of him. They didn't agree with keeping me with them... but he commanded them. Everyone obliged. "

Her father's jaw clenched at the name, but he remained silent. Idunnu hesitated for a heartbeat. "If I could show you what they looked like... it might help."

The inspector raised an eyebrow. "You want to describe them to a sketch artist?"

She shook her head. "No. I'll draw them myself."

Her parents exchanged startled looks. Even the inspector seemed surprised. "You can draw?" he asked.

Idunnu nodded firmly. "I've been taking fine art classes. My teacher says I have an eye for detail."

Within minutes, a sketchpad and pencils were brought to her. Idunnu set to work. Her hand moved swiftly, almost instinctively, as if guided by something deeper than memory. Muniru's sharp features emerged first — the angular jaw, the cold, commanding eyes. Then came the nervous man, his wide, uncertain gaze captured in trembling lines. The third man took shape last: silent, watchful, uneasy.

Idunnu stared at the page, barely recognizing the skill in the drawings. She had never seen herself as an artist; art always seemed frivolous compared to more practical pursuits. Yet the sketches before her were sharp, precise, and hauntingly accurate. How had she captured Muniru's calculating glare so perfectly? Or the nervous man's trembling fear? It was as though her mind had opened a door she never knew existed.

A chill ran down her spine, but she couldn't look away. When she finally handed the sketches to Inspector Kolade, he studied them with a look of awe.

"These are… remarkable," he murmured. "Your accuracy is extraordinary. This will help us tremendously."

Her father placed a steadying hand on her shoulder. "You've done more than enough, Idunnu. Let the police handle the rest."

But she shook her head softly. "There's something else," she said, voice weary but determined. "I checked the clock in the car. It was just after three a.m. when we stopped at that clearing. If they switched vehicles, they haven't gotten far."

Inspector Kolade straightened, already signaling to his team. "We'll set up checkpoints on every major road out of Ibarapa. With your sketches and the timing, we have a strong lead."

As officers mobilized, Idunnu's parents guided her to a quiet corner. They urged her to rest, assuring her that the worst was over. But deep inside, she felt the truth; this wasn't the end. Not yet. Her thoughts drifted to the nervous man; his hesitation, his fear.

Could that weakness be used somehow?

For now, though, her exhausted body demanded a moment of peace. She leaned against her mother's shoulder, eyelids growing heavy. Dawn had finally broken, casting soft light across the camp. Her eyelids felt heavy as she shut her eyes close.

The battle was not over. But a spark of victory had begun.

# Chapter 11:
## A New Dawn, a New Mission

The police headquarters hummed with controlled urgency. Officers moved with purpose, radios crackling with brief, sharp updates. Idunnu's sketches, now displayed on a large screen at the front of the room, had triggered instant recognition. Muniru and his crew were known troublemakers; petty criminals who had recently grown bold enough to turn to kidnapping. Their recklessness made them dangerous… but also careless.

Inspector Kolade stood before the gathered officers, pointing at the image of the thin-eyed leader. "This is Muniru," he said firmly. "Shrewd, overconfident, and increasingly desperate. These two beside him are his closest men. Their small numbers will work against them; men like these crumble when uncertainty creeps in."

Idunnu sat quietly in a corner, her parents flanking her protectively. Physically drained, she still watched the officers with a sharp attentiveness. She listened as the team mapped out their strategy: sweeping through the dense Ibarapa woodlands, establishing checkpoints at every major exit point, and searching for the camion — the truck she had overheard them mention.

But her thoughts kept drifting to the fidgety man. His trembling hands, his averted gaze, the fear in his voice.

*He's the weak link,* she thought. *He's not built for this.*

Her father touched her shoulder gently. "Idunnu," he murmured, "rest. They will handle it."

She nodded, though her heart refused to be still. *Tunde needs me. I can't rest now.* She thought to herself.

Hours later, as dusk settled over the horizon, Inspector Kolade approached the family, "We'll bring your brother home," he assured them. "Your information has given us a critical advantage."

Idunnu hesitated. Then, steadying herself, she spoke. "Inspector… the nervous man. I think he could help us. He's scared of Muniru. If we can reach him, he might talk."

Kolade regarded her carefully. "It's possible," he admitted. "But approaching him is risky. If he senses something—"

"What if **I** talk to him?" she blurted. Her parents immediately objected, but she continued quickly. "Not face-to-face. But if you can get him to speak… I'll recognize what will work. I saw how he thinks."

Kolade folded his arms thoughtfully. "A bold suggestion, Miss Idunnu. And it might give us the edge we need."

By nightfall, the operation began. A small warehouse near the Ibarapa frontier — one Idunnu had described in broad detail — became the focus. Surveillance soon confirmed movement of a truck matching her description.

Inside the mobile command van, Idunnu sat with a headset on as officers monitored intercepted calls. Suddenly, a shaky voice filled her headphones.

"We are in too deep," the nervous man whispered frantically. "Let the boy go, Muniru. Please."

Muniru's reply was ice-cold. "Shut up and obey. Disobey me, and you'll regret it."

Idunnu leaned forward. "He's breaking," she whispered. "This is our chance."

Kolade nodded and signaled his tech team. A message was discreetly sent to the nervous man's phone, appearing as an anonymous warning:

***You don't have to do this. Help us. We will protect you.***

Minutes later, surveillance cameras caught him slipping out of the warehouse, looking over his shoulder every few seconds. A plainclothes officer intercepted him and hurried him into an alley where Kolade stood waiting.

The man nearly collapsed in fear. "Please," he stuttered, "I didn't want to hurt anyone. Muniru forced me—"

Kolade cut him off sharply. "Where is the boy?"

"In the truck!" he cried. "They planned to move him at midnight… but once Muniru notices I'm gone—"

"Then we move first," Kolade said, signaling his unit.

At the back of the warehouse, they found it — a battered truck with rusting paint, parked carelessly among discarded crates. An officer yanked open the back doors and froze.

"Tunde…!"

The boy lay bound on the truck bed, weary but alive. Relief rippled through the officers.

"We've got him!" someone shouted, the words echoing into the night.

Outside, Idunnu heard the announcement over the radio. Relief slammed into her like a tidal wave. Her mother gasped, both hands flying to her mouth. Her father squeezed her shoulder firmly, voice trembling: "Go to him."

She sprinted toward the warehouse. Two officers were already helping Tunde down. When their eyes met, he managed a weak, grateful smile.

Inside the warehouse, police teams fanned out, sweeping every corner. Flashlights sliced through the darkness, revealing overturned boxes and scattered debris.

An officer suddenly called out, "Over here!" revealing a dirt-covered bag half-buried behind a heap of machinery. Inside lay several unsettling items; a yellowed map, a government-issued utility knife, and a stack of official documents sealed with state emblems. Kolade's expression darkened as he examined them, realizing this was far more than a simple kidnapping.

He radioed it in immediately. "Dispatch, we've recovered official property. Requesting forensic support."

Outside, Tunde clung to his sister. "I knew you'd come for me," he whispered, voice hoarse.

She wrapped her arms around him, sobs breaking loose. "You told me to be strong," she said through trembling breaths. "I had to."

Tunde chuckled weakly. "Looks like you did all the heavy lifting this time."

Dawn approached slowly, painting the sky in soft oranges and pinks. The siblings stood with their parents, wrapped in each other's arms as the first light of morning washed over them. The nightmare had ended; at least for now.

Nearby, officers emerged from the warehouse with Muniru and his accomplice in handcuffs. Their heads hung low, the weight of defeat settling heavily upon them. Kolade approached the family, a rare smile forming on his stern face.

"Your bravery made this possible," he told Idunnu. "You gave us exactly what we needed."

She shook her head gently. "We all did our part."

Later that evening, a nationwide broadcast aired. The police commander, standing at a podium adorned with the national emblem, addressed the country.

"Tonight," he began, "we honor the bravery and quick thinking that led to a successful operation in Ibarapa. Among our heroes is a young girl—Idunnu—whose courage and determination saved her brother and helped dismantle a dangerous criminal network." His voice remained steady as he continued, explaining that five suspects—Muniru Usman, Kayode Sanni, Godwin Lawal, Igbokwe John, and Taiwo Hassan—had been arrested. He went on to list the recovered items, including twenty-five stolen manhole covers, three vehicles, vandalized solar street lights, galvanized rods used in flyover construction, and additional tools linked to the network's operations. This network endangered countless lives and compromised public infrastructure. Their arrest is a victory for us all."

He paused, looking directly into the cameras.

"Idunnu's bravery illuminated the dangers lurking in silence. Her courage reflects the highest ideals of national service. Today, her name echoes across the country as a symbol of hope, resilience, and justice."

In their living room, Idunnu's family watched the broadcast, hearts swelling with pride. The ordeal was far from forgotten — the scars would take time to heal — but the night's victory was a step toward healing, and toward a future marked by light instead of fear.

Outside, dawn washed the Ibarapa region in a soft golden glow — the glow of new beginnings, of justice served, and of a fragile hope rising at last.

# Chapter 12:
## Lessons in Gratitude

The warm scent of jollof rice drifted through the house, wrapping the dining room in a comforting embrace. For the first time in what felt like ages, the whole family sat together at the big dinner table. The room echoed with laughter and lively chatter. Even the sunlight streaming through the windows seemed brighter, as if the house itself were celebrating Idunnu and Tunde's safe return.

Tunde sat beside Idunnu. There was a spark in his eyes that hadn't been there before—a quiet resilience. He leaned back in his chair, joking between small bites of food, speaking with his happy energy.

"You should have seen her, Tunde," their mother said, pointing toward Idunnu with a playful grin. "Your sister was like Sherlock Holmes with a pencil. The things she sketched—spot on! Those kidnappers didn't stand a chance."

Laughter erupted around the table. Idunnu felt her cheeks burn. She didn't see herself as a hero. She'd simply done what she could—what anyone would have done.

"Don't downplay it, honey," Mr. Simon, said as he raised his glass of water. "A toast to Idunnu. The artist and detective who saved the day!"

Glasses clinked as the family cheered.

"I'm very proud of you, Idunnu." Tunde grinned at her elder sister.

Idunnu smiled, though her heart fluttered with a quiet mix of pride and disbelief. Even as the laughter continued around her, her mind had already begun to drift.

Later that evening, after the dishes were washed and the house fell into a gentle hush, Idunnu slipped out to the porch. The cool night air brushed against her skin. Crickets chirped from hidden corners, the moon casting a soft glow over the quiet street. She wrapped her arms around herself and stared into the darkness, letting the memories of the past week play through her mind like a vivid film—the fear, the courage, the desperate determination.

She remembered the moment she'd decided to sketch the kidnappers. The unexpected confidence she'd felt when interpreting their whispered French conversations. How each small action—tiny pieces of knowledge she'd once dismissed—had woven themselves into the rescue of her brother.

Fine Art and French. Two subjects she had always considered pointless.

She'd never been the "theory" type. Math and science were her comfort—straightforward, predictable. Fine Art felt like a distraction. French felt like an obligation. She had never imagined they would one day become lifelines.

Her art teacher's voice echoed in her mind: "Pay attention to the details; they tell a story."

Now she understood—truly understood. The lines she drew—the tension in a brow, the tilt of a jawline, the tight curve of a smirk—had become the clues that exposed criminals. Her drawings didn't just portray faces; they revealed truths.

And French… she shook her head with a soft laugh. She used to roll her eyes at conjugations and vocabulary drills, convinced they were useless. But if she hadn't recognized words like *camion* or heard the kidnappers mention *Ibarapa*, she might never have pieced the danger together.

Knowledge had saved her brother.

A door creaked softly behind her as her mother stepped outside. She sat beside Idunnu without a word until the silence became warm. "You've been lost in thought all evening," her mother said gently. "What's on your mind?"

Idunnu hesitated, then exhaled. "I used to think Fine Art and French were useless, Mum." she confessed. "I never understood why we had to learn things we'd probably never use." A small smile tugged at her lips. "But now I see how wrong I was. Those 'pointless' things… they made all the difference."

Her mother reached over and held her hand. "That's the beauty of learning, my dear. You never know which skill will become invaluable. We give you the tools. You discover when to use them."

Idunnu nodded, her gaze drifting upward to the stars. The realization felt heavy and light at the same time. Life was unpredictable. The things she once overlooked had become her greatest strengths.

"I think I want to keep drawing," she said softly. "Not just because it helped this time… but because I enjoyed it. It felt like I was doing something meaningful."

Her mother smiled warmly. "Then follow it. When something calls to you, it's for a reason."

The following week, everything seemed different to Idunnu—sharper, more vibrant. She noticed the warm curve of her father's smile when he talked about their move. She heard the softness in her mother's voice whenever she spoke to Tunde. She took in the details of her neighborhood, the hum of familiar sounds, and the comforting chaos of home.

Because soon, they would be leaving.

The move to the UK had always felt far away—something her parents discussed in passing, something she would deal with "when the time came." But suddenly the time had come. Boxes were being brought out. Suitcases lined the hallway. Everything was changing… again.

But this time, she didn't feel helpless.

This time, she felt ready.

She looked at the sketches on her bedroom wall—once assignments, now achievements. Her old French workbook sat at the edge of her desk, dog-eared and worn, but now filled with purpose instead of frustration.

She imagined her first day at her new school—the art room smelling of paint and charcoal, the French classroom echoing with words she now respected, even cherished. She imagined herself walking confidently into a space where no one knew her story yet… but where she would write a new one.

As the boxes piled up and her room slowly emptied, a bittersweet ache settled inside her. Leaving Nigeria meant leaving everything she knew—the mango trees, the sounds of okadas at dusk, the warmth of neighbors greeting her by name. But she was carrying more than memories. She carried lessons, courage, and a new understanding of herself.

"You'll do wonderfully," her mother said as she folded clothes into the suitcase. "You'll show them who you are."

Her father added softly, "This move is a fresh start for all of us, Idunnu. Not just you."

His words settled into the quiet space between them, warm and steady, and she held them close like a shield against the uncertainty pressing on her chest.

"Are… are you guys excited to leave?" she asked. Her voice was barely above a whisper, as though speaking too loudly would make the truth more real.

Mrs. Adebayo reached over and brushed a loose curl from Idunnu's cheek. "Of course," she said with a gentle smile. "We all are. It's a big change for the family. But a good one." She paused, tilting her head. "Are you not?"

"I guess," Idunnu said with a small shrug. The word tasted hesitant.

Her eyes drifted across the room—the framed pictures, the familiar curtains, the soft hum of the neighborhood outside. Everything she had ever known. Everything she had grown up breathing.

"I'll miss this," she admitted, her voice tightening. "I'll miss… all of this."

Her mother didn't ask what she meant. She already knew. She had seen it in her daughter's eyes ever since they shared the news:
Idunnu wasn't just talking about a house, or a street, or a city.

She was talking about home.

Her Nigeria.

The soil that shaped her, the people who carried her, the life that stretched behind her like a vivid, irreplaceable tapestry.

Her mother reached for her hand and squeezed it. Her father stepped closer, resting a reassuring hand on her shoulder. For a moment, the three of them stood together, not as individuals facing a move, but as a family shouldering a transition—one that would change all their lives.

And even though they were leaving, Nigeria would always live inside them.

Always.

# Chapter 13:
# Whole New World

The airport buzzed with life—luggage wheels clattering, conversation in dozens of voices, announcements echoing off the high ceilings. Yet, as Idunnu walked beside her family through the bright terminal, a calm settled over her. The chaos around them seemed distant, almost muted, as if the world had narrowed to this single, profound moment.

She glanced at each of them: her father, steady and composed, eyes kind and reassuring; her mother, gently holding Tunde's hand, warmth radiating like a quiet shield; Tunde, eyes wide with awe, absorbing every detail of the bustling terminal.

The weight of leaving pressed on all of them, heavy with the change, yet comforting in the shared presence of one another. They were not just leaving a house—they were leaving a lifetime of memories, streets and smells and voices that had shaped them, the rhythm of life that pulsed through their neighborhood.

Idunnu felt a lump rise in her throat. Every corner of this airport seemed to whisper of home—the smell of warm pastries in the café, the soft echo of Nigerian Pidgin blending with English, the distant laughter of children playing while their parents dragged luggage. Each sound was a reminder of her life she was about to leave behind.

One by one, the family embraced their friends who came to drop by. Her parents, long and lingering, exchanged silent words in their hugs. Her father's hand rested briefly on his friend's shoulder. Her mother's eyes glimmered with worry and love wrapped around her like a cloak. The family and friends shared small, quiet embraces, their usual teasing absent as they felt the gravity of the moment.

As they gathered their belongings and moved toward the boarding gate, Idunnu noticed small details she had never paid attention to before—the shine of the airport tiles, the polished metal of the luggage trolleys, the soft hum of the escalators carrying travelers to departure halls. Each detail seemed to echo with a kind of permanence she wasn't ready to leave behind.

The terminal filled with the announcement:

"Flight 228 to London Heathrow is now boarding." Heartbeats quickened. Passports in hand, the family moved forward together.

Sliding into her seat by the window, Idunnu fastened her seatbelt and glanced around. Her family settled beside her—her mother and father in the row ahead, Tunde tucked beside her. Outside, Nigeria stretched beneath them in warm, earthy tones: red clay rooftops glinting in the sun, green patches of farmland, winding streets where life carried on in familiar rhythm. People moved like threads in a living tapestry, weaving the home she was leaving behind.

The engines roared to life, vibrating through the cabin. The plane rolled forward, a subtle tremor running through the floor and into her chest. Within minutes, the runway blurred, and the aircraft tilted upward, gaining altitude slowly, gracefully, powerfully. Idunnu pressed her palm to the window, feeling the hum of the engines, the world below receding with every second.

She could hear her mother quietly humming a familiar song, a lullaby from her childhood, and it wrapped around her like a warm blanket. Her father's hand rested on Tunde's shoulder, steadying him as he stared wide-eyed at the shrinking city.

Tears pricked her eyes, but her heart was full. They were not just leaving one country for another—they were rising together, stepping into a life brimming with possibility, learning, and discovery. She thought back to the last weeks: the moments of fear and courage, the lessons she had once dismissed—Fine Art, French—that had become her lifelines, the rescue of Tunde, the sketches that had revealed truths, the small victories that had shaped her. All of it had brought her family to this threshold.

A quiet pride swelled in her chest. They had survived, learned, and grown. Strength, creativity, and courage had intertwined in ways she could never have imagined.

The clouds came to meet them as the sun streaked gold across the horizon. For the first time, Idunnu exhaled completely, allowing herself to embrace the uncertainty, the thrill, and the quiet beauty of adventure ahead. She reached into her bag and pulled out her sketchbook and pencil, her hands finding comfort in their familiar weight.

Outside the window, the world expanded endlessly. Inside her, a new chapter began. Together, the family was stepping into it, hand in hand, hearts aligned.

As the plane climbed higher, Idunnu began to draw, tracing the journey she had traveled, the lessons learned, and the path ahead. Each line, each shadow, each stroke a reminder: nothing was wasted, and every step, every shared moment, had led them here.

Her eyes lifted from the page to the horizon beyond the clouds. They were leaving home—but they were not leaving themselves behind. They were ready.

And with that, she drew.

# Chapter 14:
# A Sky Full of Beginnings

The moment Idunnu stepped out of the plane, a cool rush of air wrapped around her like an unexpected embrace. It wasn't harsh; just different. Crisp and sharp. Almost curious, as though the new world itself was leaning in to study her.

Heathrow hummed with movement. People glided past her in every direction, luggage wheels rolling like waves, voices blending into a soft, steady buzz. Announcements echoed overhead in accents she wasn't used to; rounder vowels, quicker syllables, strange music in each word. She adjusted her backpack on her shoulder, taking it all in.

She glanced around at her family—her parents, and Tunde—walking beside her, all carrying their luggage and staying close together. She wasn't alone. None of them were. The journey was theirs together, a collective step into the unknown.

*This is real,* she thought. *I'm here.*

She followed the stream of passengers through the bright terminal alongside her family. Idunnu's eyes flicking from one unfamiliar detail to another; the polished floors reflecting rows of lights, screens announcing flights to cities she had only seen in textbooks, faces of people from places she had never imagined. Outside the glass walls, England lay under a blanket of soft grey; muted tones, calm and quiet. A light drizzle tapped against the windows, delicate and rhythmic, like gentle fingers welcoming her to a place that felt both distant and astonishingly close.

When she reached the baggage carousel, her suitcase appeared with a slow rotation. She pulled the heavy case off the belt and steadied herself.

I can do this, she reminded herself.

Her parents led the family through the sliding doors into the arrivals area. Immediately, the cold hit them—not the indoor softness, but a full, brisk chill that kissed their cheeks and seeped through their sleeves. Idunnu pulled her jacket tighter and inhaled deeply. The air smelled different here—cleaner, cooler, tinged with rain and something metallic.

Her aunt, Aunty Victoria, spotted them before they had time to search. "I-dun-nu!" she exclaimed, her voice warm and bright against the chilly air.

Idunnu felt her chest loosen as she fell into the hug.

"You've grown," her aunt said, holding her at arm's length. "And look at you, all brave and grown-up!"

Her father smiled, shaking hands briefly with Aunty Victoria. "Thank you for having us," he said. "It's a big change for all of us, but we're glad to be here."

Her mother nodded, adjusting Tunde's scarf. "Yes, it's quite the journey, but we trust you'll help us settle in."

Tunde bounced slightly on his heels, tugging at his mother's sleeve. "Aunty Victoria , are there any parks nearby? And can we explore the shops?" he asked eagerly, his eyes wide with curiosity.

Aunty Victoria laughed softly, crouching down to his level. "Oh, plenty of parks, Tunde. And the shops... well, we'll take it slow. There's so much to see. Don't worry, I'll show you everything. You'll get used to it in no time, my love."

His parents exchanged a look, both relieved and amused by his excitement. "Just don't run off too far, okay?" his mother said, ruffling his hair. "We need to stick together at first."

"Promise!" Tunde said, though a grin spread across his face. "I'll behave… mostly."

Idunnu watched them, feeling a sense of warmth wash over her. Even though everything was new and different, her family was here—together—and that made the unfamiliar world feel just a little bit safer.

They walked toward the car park together, the cold breeze tugging gently at Idunnu's braids. Cars flashed by, sleek and quiet, headlights scattering across wet pavement.

Inside the car, Idunnu pressed her forehead to the window as the city blurred past: rows of brick houses with chimneys, buses the size of small buildings, people walking briskly with umbrellas. Everything moved differently here—faster, more precise, yet oddly quiet.

It took the family two weeks to find a school that could enroll Idunnu and Tunde. They stayed in temporary accommodation, exploring local shops, parks, this place called Hanley and quiet corners of the neighborhood to pass the time. Each day, she clung to her sketchbook, drawing and practicing French, imagining her new life while learning to navigate this strange city.

During one of those nights, her uncle Segun, also known as Bushana in America, called. He spoke warmly to her parents about how proud he was of her bravery, though Idunnu was asleep and missed the call. Her parents told her the next morning, smiling, that he had sent her $100. She was thrilled, hearing how he praised her as a great Wagadugu descendant, saying she exhibited her grandfather's exceptional courage.

Finally, the day came when she received her acceptance to a local school. She dressed carefully, smoothing her new uniform and tying her shoes with slow, steady hands. Unlike her Nigerian school uniform, which had always been a bright blue pinafore with a crisp white blouse and matching blue socks, this one was more formal and muted: a navy blazer with the school crest stitched neatly on the pocket, a white button-up shirt, a plaid skirt, and navy knee-high socks. Even the shoes were different—polished black leather instead of the simple sandals she was used to.

She took a moment to adjust her blazer, noticing how stiff and unfamiliar it felt compared to the soft cotton of her uniform, but she straightened her shoulders and smoothed down her skirt. Today was her first day at school.

As she stepped through the school gates, cold air brushed her face, but her heart thudded with heat—anticipation, nervousness, and a spark of courage she carried from home.

Students spilled across the grounds, chatting in fast English, their accents twisting and tumbling over each other like swirling ribbons. Many glanced at her, some with curiosity, others with barely a second thought. Idunnu felt the weight of every stare; she was new, different, and instantly noticeable in a sea of familiar faces.

Her chest tightened—just for a moment—before she reminded herself of the sketchbook in her bag. The French notebook. The strength she didn't know she possessed until she had needed it. She straightened her shoulders and stepped forward.

The hallways were bright and echoing, lockers clanging here and there. Students moved in groups, whispering and laughing, some turning to give her strange looks as she passed, their eyes narrowing or widening at her presence. She tried to ignore it, but it prickled at her skin like tiny sparks.

Then, as she rounded a corner, a girl collided with her shoulder. Idunnu's sketchbook tumbled to the floor with a soft thud.

"Oh! Watch where you're going!" someone called, and a few others snickered. Faces turned, some amused, some indifferent. Idunnu bent quickly to pick up her book, cheeks burning.

Flustered, she made her way to the nearest bathroom to gather herself. The walls smelled faintly of soap and cleaning spray, and the noise of chatter outside seemed to fade. Just as she washed her hands, a voice interrupted her thoughts.

"Hi! You're new, right?" A girl with a warm smile leaned against the sink. Her brown eyes were kind, and there was an easy confidence about her. "I'm Mia. Want me to show you around?"

Idunnu looked up, surprised, and nodded.

"Yeah… I'd like that," she said, a small smile breaking through.

And just like that, the world widened again. The cold didn't feel so sharp. The strange looks didn't feel so heavy. This place—vast, unfamiliar, a little intimidating—was hers to explore, to learn, to grow into.

Her new chapter had begun.

And she was ready for it all.

# Chapter 15:
# A Table Full of Eyes

Idunnu noticed it in the mirror first.

Not in a dramatic way—no sudden shock, no cinematic moment—but in the quiet, unguarded second when she leaned closer to knot her tie and her own face looked back at her without permission.

Her cheeks had hollowed slightly. The skin beneath her eyes carried a faint shadow, like she hadn't slept in days. Even her lips looked paler than usual, as if the color had been gently drained out of her. She blinked, then forced her expression into something neutral.

Behind her, her mother moved through the room with the soft efficiency of routine, smoothing a sleeve, checking a button, adjusting the collar of Idunnu's blazer.

"You're getting so slim," Mrs. Adebayo said, not worried. "This school is making you serious."

Idunnu's throat tightened. She kept her eyes on the mirror and lifted her chin a fraction, as if confidence could be worn like the uniform.

"I'm fine, Mummy," she said.

Mrs. Adebayo smiled, satisfied with the answer. "Just don't overwork yourself. You're always reading. Always writing. Always trying."

Idunnu smiled back because it was easier than explaining. Because the truth would sound strange in the morning light.

At home, eating was private. Safe. Nobody watched her chew. Nobody waited for the moment her throat tightened and she had to open her mouth wider to breathe through it. Nobody lifted a phone like a spotlight. But at school, it had become a game.

She picked up her bag, checked her phone, and followed her mother out.

Outside, the air was cold enough to wake her fully. She inhaled, steadying herself, and walked to the bus stop with careful steps. The street smelled like damp pavement and exhaust. Her stomach was empty, but she had learned how to treat emptiness like background noise.

By the time she reached school, the building was already alive—voices, footsteps, lockers clanging, and laughter bouncing off walls. She moved through it like someone passing through water, trying not to disturb anything.

Mia found her near the lockers. "Morning," Mia said, bright as always.

Idunnu nodded. "Morning."

Mia's smile faltered slightly as her eyes scanned Idunnu's face. "Are you okay?"

"I'm fine," Idunnu said again, the phrase sliding out automatically.

Zainab and Kemi joined them a moment later. Zainab had her book tucked under her arm. Kemi carried a small snack packet she didn't open. They walked together to class, and for a few minutes Idunnu almost believed she could make it through the day without anything happening.

Lunch period was when everything changed. The cafeteria was loud, as always—metal chairs scraping, trays clattering, voices overlapping until the room became one steady roar. But Idunnu noticed the way sound shifted when *they* entered.

The girls.

They always arrived like they owned the air.

Four of them, moving in a tight group, uniforms altered just enough to show they could get away with it. Their laughter was sharp, practiced, and slightly too loud—like a warning disguised as fun. Their names traveled through the school the way rumors did: quick, careless, and certain. Sienna was the leader. Pretty in a polished way, eyes always alert, smile always half a second away from cruelty. Chloe followed her like an echo; quick to laugh, quicker to repeat whatever Sienna started. Amanda was quieter, but that didn't make her kinder. She watched more than she spoke, and when she did speak, it landed. Shannon was the one who pretended she didn't care, which somehow made her the most dangerous. She did things with a shrug, like harm was accidental.

The first time they'd targeted Idunnu, she hadn't understood what it was. She'd thought it was curiosity. A joke. A misunderstanding. Now she knew better.

Idunnu sat with Mia, Zainab, and Kemi at their usual table. Her hands rested in her lap. No lunchbox. No food. Just a bottle of water she kept twisting open and closed.

Mia noticed immediately. "Idunnu," she said quietly, leaning closer. "Where's your lunch?""

It wasn't just hunger that made her stomach twist.

The first week she'd tried to eat normally, she'd learned the hard way that her body didn't cooperate. Idunnu had a narrow food passage, and sometimes swallowing took effort. She had to take smaller bites, chew longer, and—worst of all—open her mouth a little wider than other people did, just to breathe and work the food down without choking.

Sienna had noticed.

Not in a concerned way. In the way predators notice a limp.

A day later, Idunnu had heard the sharp click of a phone camera from the next table. Then another. She'd looked up and seen Chloe's screen angled toward her, the lens pointed like a tiny weapon.

That afternoon, the photo found her anyway.

A blurred close-up of her face mid-bite, mouth open, eyes half-squeezed as she tried to swallow—captioned with laughing emojis and a word that made her skin burn. The image had been passed around like a joke no one needed to explain. By the next morning, people she didn't even know were looking at her like they were trying to match her real face to the ugly frozen moment.

Since then, food at school had stopped being food.

It was evidence.

So she learned to keep her lips closed. To sip water. To swallow nothing in public. To make herself smaller in every way she could.

"Well, look at that," Sienna said, stopping beside their table as if she'd been invited. "She's doing that thing again."

Chloe's phone was already half-raised, camera ready as giggled. "The starving thing."

Idunnu's throat tightened on instinct—her body remembering the last photo, the last caption, the way laughter could live forever on a screen.

Shannon leaned in, eyes scanning the table like she was inspecting evidence. "No food today? Are you on some kind of… diet?"

Amanda's gaze flicked to Idunnu's face. "Or is it just that her food is too embarrassing to bring now?" Their laughter wasn't loud enough to draw a teacher. It was loud enough to draw attention.

Idunnu's chest tightened. She stared at the table, at the scratches in the surface, at anything that wasn't their faces.

Mia stood up. "Can you just leave her alone?"

Sienna smiled sweetly. "We're not doing anything. We're just talking."

Chloe added, "Yeah, Mia. Don't be so dramatic."

Mia's jaw clenched. "You're doing it on purpose."

But before they left, Sienna leaned closer to Idunnu, lowering her voice just enough to make it feel private. Idunnu caught the quick flash of a screen—Shannon angling her phone toward her lap, lens facing up. Like they were ready in case Idunnu made the mistake of taking a bite.

"You know," she said, "if you don't eat, you'll faint. And then everyone will really have something to talk about." Her smile deepened. "Maybe we'll even get a better picture this time."

Idunnu's stomach dropped.

Sienna straightened and walked away, her group following, laughter trailing behind them like perfume.

Mia sat back down, furious. "I swear—"

"It's fine," Idunnu whispered.

"It's not fine," Mia said.

But Idunnu didn't answer. Because if she spoke, her voice might break. And once it broke, she wasn't sure she could put it back together. The rest of the day moved slowly, like the school had been filled with thicker air.

Sometimes, she caught herself thinking about how far she had already come—how leaving Nigeria had not been a simple move, but she survived. How she had survived the fear that once hovered over her and her brother, the stories of kidnappers that made every outing feel like a risk, every goodbye feel too long. She remembered the relief of being pulled out of that danger, the pride she'd felt in her own bravery, and the way she'd clung to the few things that made her feel like herself: French words that tasted elegant on her tongue now, and art—lines and colors that let her speak when she didn't have the language for everything else. She had imagined this new life as a beginning, a widening of the world. She hadn't imagined that safety could still come with a different kind of threat and one that didn't chase her through streets, but cornered her in a cafeteria, quietly, every day.

And yet, sitting there, she felt her body disagree with every brave story she told herself. Suddenly, the room seemed to thicken around her, the noise turning distant and uneven, like it was coming from underwater. She noticed her heartbeat grew louder than the voices, louder than the scraping chairs, louder than the laughter.

*Is this normal? What's happening?* She thought to herself.

She took a slow breath and tried to steady her hands, but her fingers felt strangely light, as if they didn't belong to her. The teacher's voice droned on, but the words blurred. Idunnu tried to focus on the board. She tried to keep her breathing steady.

Her vision narrowed as black spots gathered at the edges like ink. She pressed her palms against the desk, trying to anchor herself. The wood felt too smooth, too far away, as if her hands belonged to someone else. Suddenly, her heart began to pound— loud and frantic—like her body was trying to warn her of something her mind had refused to acknowledge.

"Idunnu?" someone called.

She blinked her eyes, and tried to look at the origin of the sound but it felt distant. She tried to answer, but her tongue felt heavy. Her mouth was dry. Her limbs were weak, as if the strength had been quietly draining out of her for days and had finally reached the bottom.

The room tilted; sharply. Her chair scraped as she slid forward. The desk edge caught her ribs. Then the floor rose up too fast.

A dull, sickening thud.

Gasps erupted. A chair toppled. Shoes scuffed. Someone shouted her name—Mia's voice, sharp with fear.

"Get the nurse!" the teacher barked.

Idunnu heard none of it.

For the first time in weeks, she felt nothing at all.

When Idunnu opened her eyes, the world smelled like antiseptic and something faintly sweet—like cough syrup. She was lying on a narrow bed with a thin paper sheet beneath her. The ceiling tiles above her were dotted with tiny holes. A clock ticked loudly on the wall, each second too deliberate.

A woman's voice cut through the fog. "Idunnu. Can you hear me?"

Idunnu turned her head slightly. The nurse stood beside her, middle-aged, hair pulled back, expression calm but watchful. She swallowed as her throat felt dry. "Yes."

"Good," the nurse said. "Don't sit up too fast."

Idunnu tried anyway, then immediately regretted it as she noticed the room swayed. The nurse pressed a hand gently to her shoulder. "Easy." She checked her pulse, then her blood pressure, then shone a small light into her eyes.

"How old are you?" the nurse asked.

"Twelve," Idunnu whispered.

"Have you eaten today?"

Idunnu hesitated.

The nurse's eyes stayed on her face.

Idunnu nodded quickly. "Yes."

"What did you eat?" The question was simple, but it landed like a trap.

Idunnu's mind scrambled. "I… I had something this morning."

The nurse didn't move. "What?"

Idunnu's cheeks warmed. "Toast."

The nurse's expression didn't change, but something in her gaze sharpened. "And lunch?"

Idunnu swallowed again. "I wasn't hungry."

The nurse exhaled softly, like she'd heard this before. "Idunnu, fainting is not normal. Especially not at twelve."

Idunnu stared at her hands. They looked smaller than usual, the knuckles slightly prominent. The nurse pulled a chair closer and sat.

"I'm going to ask you again, and I need you to be honest. Have you been eating properly?"

Idunnu's mouth opened, ready to say yes. But the word wouldn't come. Her eyes stung suddenly, and she hated herself for it. She blinked hard, forcing the tears back.

"I… I eat," she said, but it sounded weak even to her.

The nurse nodded slowly, as if she'd expected that answer. "Okay. Here's what we're going to do. You're going to drink some water. Then you're going to eat something small—something with sugar and something with salt. And then I'm calling your parents."

Idunnu's head snapped up. "No."

The nurse's voice stayed calm. "Yes."

Idunnu's chest tightened. "Please. I'm fine. I just— I stood up too fast."

The nurse looked at her for a long moment.

Then she said, gently but firmly, "Idunnu, you collapsed in class. That is not 'stood up too fast.'"

Idunnu's fingers curled into the sheet.

The nurse stood. "I'm going to step out and make a call. You stay here."

Idunnu's heart began to race again—not from faintness this time, but fear. Fear of her mother's face when she heard. Fear of questions she couldn't answer without opening everything up.

The nurse walked to her desk and picked up the phone as Idunnu sat up slowly, carefully. She swung her legs over the side of the bed, feet touching the cold floor. The nurse's voice carried through the room, low and professional.

"Hello, is this Mrs. Adebayo? Yes, this is the school nurse..."

Idunnu stood. The room tilted immediately. She grabbed the edge of the bed, breathing shallowly.

The nurse turned, eyes narrowing. "Idunnu—sit down."

"I'm okay," Idunnu said, but her voice sounded far away.

She took one step toward the door. The floor seemed to slide. Her ears rang.

The nurse's voice sharpened. "Idunnu!"

Idunnu tried to reach the wall, tried to steady herself…but her body gave up again. She could feel her knees buckling as she hit the floor with a soft, terrible thud.

And this time, she didn't even have the strength to be embarrassed.

Only the distant sound of the nurse calling her name, and the phone still open, her mother's voice faintly audible on the other end.

# Chapter 16:
# The Recovery

Idunnu woke to a ceiling she didn't recognize.

It wasn't the familiar pale paint of her bedroom, or the soft yellow light that usually slipped through the curtains in the morning. This ceiling was white and too bright, broken into neat squares with a strip of fluorescent light humming above her like an insect that refused to die.

For a moment, she didn't remember where she was.

Then the smell hit her—clean, sharp antiseptic with something faintly sweet underneath—and the memory returned in pieces: the classroom tilting, the floor rising too fast, Mia's voice shouting her name, the nurse's hands on her shoulder, the second fall that had stolen even her embarrassment.

Her throat felt dry. Her body felt heavy, as if someone had filled her limbs with sand.

A monitor beeped steadily somewhere to her left.

Idunnu turned her head slowly. A thin tube ran into the back of her hand, taped down with clear dressing. A bag of fluid hung from a metal stand, dripping with patient rhythm.

She stared at it, blinking.

So it was real.

A chair scraped softly.

Her mother was there, sitting close to the bed. Mrs. Adebayo's face looked tired in a way Idunnu had never seen—tired past makeup, past routine, past the calm efficiency that usually held their home together. When Mrs. Adebayo noticed Idunnu's eyes open, she leaned forward so quickly her handbag slid off her lap.

"Idunnu," she whispered, as if saying her name too loudly might make her disappear again.

Idunnu tried to speak. Her voice came out rough. "Mummy."

Mrs. Adebayo exhaled, a shaky breath she tried to hide by smoothing Idunnu's blanket. "Don't talk too much. The nurse said you need rest."

Idunnu's eyes drifted to the IV again. "I…"

"You fainted," Mrs. Adebayo said, and her voice tightened on the word. "Twice."

Idunnu swallowed. Even that small movement made her throat ache.

Mrs. Adebayo brushed her fingers over Idunnu's hair, careful, like she was handling something fragile. "You scared me."

Idunnu wanted to say she was sorry. But sorry felt too small for the way her mother's eyes shone, for the way her mother's hand trembled against the blanket.

Instead, she whispered, "I didn't mean to."

Her mother gave a short nod, like she was trying to accept that. Then she looked at Idunnu's face—really looked. "You've been losing weight," she said quietly.

Idunnu's stomach tightened.

"You told me you were fine," Mrs. Adebayo continued. "You told me it was school making you serious."

Idunnu turned her gaze away, toward the window. Outside, the sky was the flat grey of England mornings, the kind that made everything look like it was waiting.

"I am fine," Idunnu said automatically.

Mrs. Adebayo didn't answer right away. She stood and walked to the foot of the bed, then back again, like her body needed motion to keep her from breaking. Then she sat down and spoke with a calm that sounded practiced—like she'd borrowed it from somewhere.

"Idunnu," she said, "the doctor said fainting like this doesn't happen because you 'stood up too fast.' It happens when your body has been running on empty."

Idunnu's fingers curled against the sheet. Mrs. Adebayo leaned closer. "Have you been eating?"

Idunnu hesitated and the pause was enough. Her mother's eyes softened, but her voice stayed firm. "Tell me the truth."

Idunnu opened her mouth. The words rose up like a tide. But so did the shame. She pictured the cafeteria. The scrape of chairs. The way Sienna's smile always arrived before her cruelty. The click of a phone camera that sounded harmless until it wasn't.

Idunnu swallowed hard. "I… I try," she said.

Mrs. Adebayo's brows drew together. "Try?"

Idunnu stared at her own hand, the tape holding the IV in place. Her knuckles looked too sharp. "It's not that I don't want to," she whispered.

Mrs. Adebayo waited.

Idunnu's throat tightened. "At school… I can't."

"Why?"

Idunnu's eyes stung. She blinked fast, refusing to cry. Crying would make it real in a way she wasn't ready for. But it was already real. "They…" Idunnu began.

Mrs. Adebayo reached for her hand, careful around the IV, and held it anyway.

"There are girls."

Mrs. Adebayo's grip tightened. "Girls?"

Idunnu nodded once. The words came out in pieces at first. "They sit near us at lunch. They… they watch me."

Mrs. Adebayo's face hardened, confusion turning into something sharper. "Watch you for what?"

Idunnu's cheeks warmed. Heat crawled up her neck. She hated how childish it sounded, like she was complaining about nothing. But it wasn't nothing.

"I have… I have a narrow passage. When I eat, sometimes I have to take small bites. I have to chew longer. And sometimes…" Her voice dropped to almost nothing. "Sometimes I have to open my mouth wider to breathe and swallow properly."

Mrs. Adebayo's eyes widened slightly, not with disgust—never that—but with sudden understanding.

"They noticed."

Mrs. Adebayo's lips parted. "Who noticed?"

Idunnu forced herself to say it. "The mean girls. Sienna and her friends. They take pictures. When I'm eating. When my mouth is open."

Mrs. Adebayo went still.

"They… they send them around. They laugh. They make it look like I'm… like I'm disgusting." The tears came anyway, hot and unwanted. Idunnu wiped them quickly with the back of her free hand, ashamed.

Mrs. Adebayo's face changed in an instant. The tiredness disappeared; something steadier replaced it. "Who has these pictures?"

Idunnu shook her head. "I don't know. It's… it's everywhere."

"And you stopped eating because of this?"

"It was easier," she whispered. "If I don't eat, they don't have anything to take."

Mrs. Adebayo's eyes glistened. "Oh, my baby."

"I didn't want you to worry." Idunnu's throat tightened.

Mrs. Adebayo shook her head once, firm. "That is my job. To worry. To protect you." She leaned forward and kissed Idunnu's forehead. Then she sat back, and her voice turned practical in a way Idunnu recognized—her mother's way of turning fear into action. "Listen to me," Mrs. Adebayo said. "You are not going back to that school without this being handled. Do you hear me?"

Idunnu's eyes widened. "Mummy—"

"No," Mrs. Adebayo cut in gently. "No more hiding. No more carrying this alone."

Idunnu stared at her. Part of her felt relief so sharp it almost hurt. Another part felt terror because telling meant consequences. Telling meant Sienna's eyes on her. Telling meant being the girl who couldn't handle it.

Mrs. Adebayo squeezed her hand. "I'm going to speak to the principal."

"Please don't make it worse."

"It is already worse. You are in a hospital bed."

Idunnu closed her eyes.

When she opened them again, the nurse was stepping into the room.

She was the same woman from the school office, calm and watchful, but now she wore a hospital badge clipped to her uniform.

"Good morning," the nurse said. "How are we feeling?"

Idunnu tried to answer, but her mother spoke first.

"She's been bullied," Mrs. Adebayo said.

The words landed like a stone. The nurse's expression changed—no shock, no disbelief. Just a quiet seriousness.

"I'm sorry to hear that," she said. Then she looked at Idunnu. "Thank you for telling your mum."

Idunnu stared at the blanket.

The nurse checked the IV, then the monitor, then handed Idunnu a small cup of water.

"Small sips," she instructed.

Idunnu obeyed.

The next two days blurred into a slow rhythm. A doctor with kind eyes explaining electrolytes and dehydration in a voice that made it sound like science, not shame. A tray with toast, then soup, then a banana. Idunnu ate in tiny bites, her throat still cautious, her body still learning that food didn't have to be a battlefield.

Her mother stayed as much as she could, leaving only to go home for clothes and to make phone calls in the corridor with her voice low and controlled. Idunnu didn't ask who she called. She didn't need to.

On the third morning, Mrs. Adebayo returned with her coat buttoned and her face set.

“I spoke to the principal,” she said.

Idunnu’s heart jumped. “What did he say?”

Mrs. Adebayo sat down. “He said he wants to meet us. Today.”

Idunnu’s mouth went dry.

Mrs. Adebayo reached into her bag and pulled out a small notebook.

“I wrote down what you told me,” she said. “Names. What they did. When it started. We are going to be clear.”

Idunnu stared at the notebook. It felt strange—her pain turned into bullet points.

But it also felt powerful.

Like proof.

# Chapter 17:
# The Phoenix

The principal's office smelled like coffee and old paper. Idunnu sat beside her mother, hands folded tightly in her lap. The principal sat across from them, a man with a neat tie and tired eyes that sharpened when he listened.

"Idunnu," he said gently, "I'm sorry this happened to you."

Idunnu nodded, unable to speak.

Mrs. Adebayo did not waste time. She explained everything. The lunchroom. The phones. The pictures. The captions. The fainting. The hospital. Idunnu watched the principal's face change as the story unfolded. When her mother finished, the principal exhaled slowly.

"This is serious," he said.

Mrs. Adebayo's voice stayed calm, but her eyes were fierce. "What will you do?"

The principal leaned forward. "We will investigate immediately. We will speak to the students involved. We will contact their parents. And we will put measures in place so Idunnu is safe."

Idunnu's throat tightened. "Safe how?"

The principal looked at her. "You will not sit near them in class. You will not be placed in group work with them. At lunch, we will ensure staff supervision around your table. And if there are images, we will require deletion and treat any sharing as a disciplinary issue."

Mrs. Adebayo nodded once. "Good."

The principal continued, "We also have a school counsellor. I'd like to offer you weekly check-ins, Idunnu. Not because you did anything wrong, but because you shouldn't have to carry this alone."

Idunnu's eyes stung as she nodded.

The principal's voice hardened slightly. "And there will be consequences for the students responsible."

Mrs. Adebayo's shoulders eased, just a fraction. Idunnu felt something loosen in her chest. Not relief. Not yet.

But the first crack in the wall.

**

By the end of the week, Idunnu was discharged. She walked out of the hospital slowly, her mother's hand steady at her elbow. The air outside was cold and clean. Idunnu inhaled deeply; her body still felt fragile but it was hers again.

At home, her mother made food that smelled like comfort—rice, stew, warm bread. Idunnu ate without eyes on her. She ate without fear. She slept. She drew. She wrote a few lines in her notebook that didn't feel like pain, just truth. And each day, she felt a little stronger.

The morning she returned to school, Idunnu stood in front of the mirror again. Her cheeks still looked slimmer than before but her eyes looked clearer. She adjusted her tie, breathing slowly.

Behind her, her mother watched. "You don't have to be brave all at once,"

Idunnu nodded. "I know."

Mrs. Adebayo stepped forward and straightened Idunnu's collar with gentle hands. "But you are not alone."

Idunnu swallowed. "I told."

Mrs. Adebayo smiled softly. "And that was brave."

School looked the same but Idunnu felt different walking through the gates. Mia spotted her first. Her face lit up, and she ran the last few steps like she couldn't help herself.

"Idunnu!" Mia hugged her carefully, like she was afraid to break her.

Zainab and Kemi came right behind, both smiling with relief. "We missed you," Kemi said.

Zainab's voice was softer than usual. "Are you okay?"

Idunnu nodded. "I'm getting there."

They walked together toward the lockers as Idunnu's heart thudded. Not from weakness but from memory. Then the air shifted. Idunnu felt it before she saw them.

Sienna stood a few steps away with Chloe, Amanda, and Jade.

They weren't laughing. They weren't loud. For once, they didn't look like they owned the hallway. Sienna's eyes flicked to Idunnu's face, then away.

"Idunnu," she said.

Mia's posture changed instantly but Idunnu didn't move. Instead, she waited.

Sienna swallowed. "We... we need to say sorry."

Chloe nodded quickly. "We're sorry."

Amanda's voice was quiet. "What we did was wrong."

Shannon looked down, then up. "The pictures. The comments. All of it."

Idunnu's stomach tightened.

"We deleted them. The principal spoke to our parents."

Chloe added, "We're not going to bother you anymore."

"You shouldn't have in the first place."

Sienna flinched, but she didn't argue. Idunnu felt the silence stretch. She took a slow breath.

"I hear you," Idunnu said, her voice steady. "And I accept your apology."

Sienna's shoulders loosened slightly but dunnu didn't stop there. "But we're not friends," she continued, calm and clear. "And we won't be. You don't get to hurt someone and then act like it's nothing once you're told to stop."

The hallway seemed to go quieter. Idunnu held Sienna's gaze.

"Keep it respectful. Keep your distance. And don't do it to anyone else."

They stepped back, letting the space open again and Idunnu exhaled slowly.

Mia leaned closer. "That was perfect," she whispered.

Idunnu didn't smile fully, but something in her chest eased. She turned toward her locker. The metal was cool beneath her fingertips. And for the first time in a long time, she felt like she could stand in the middle of school without folding in on herself.

Not because the world had suddenly become kind.

But because she had finally stopped carrying it alone.

# Chapter 18:
# A Story Worth Telling

Idunnu didn't wake up hungry the way she used to before everything went wrong. But she woke up steady. That was new.

The morning light in her room was thin and grey, the kind that made London look like it was holding its breath. Idunnu sat up slowly, letting her body catch up with her mind. Her chest rose and fell without that sharp panic she'd carried for weeks. Her legs didn't feel like they would fold under her the moment she stood.

On her bedside table, a glass of water waited—half full, proof that she'd been learning to take care of herself in small, consistent ways.

She swung her feet onto the floor and stood. In the mirror, she still looked like someone who had been through something. But she also looked like someone who had survived it.

Her cheeks weren't as hollow as before. The shadows beneath her eyes had softened. There was still a quietness in her face, a carefulness, but it wasn't emptiness anymore. It was caution. It was healing.

Behind her, the house was already awake. She could hear the faint clink of a spoon against a mug, the low murmur of her parents' voices.

Idunnu pulled on her uniform, tied her tie, and paused for a second with her fingers resting on the knot.

*I'm going back,* she thought.

Not just to the building.

To herself.

Breakfast used to feel like a test but now it felt like a choice. Her mother placed a small plate in front of her—toast cut into neat triangles, a boiled egg, and a cup of tea. Nothing dramatic. Nothing forced.

Mrs. Adebayo sat across from her, watching without making it obvious. Idunnu picked up the toast and took a bite. Her throat still required patience. She chewed slowly, swallowed carefully, and breathed through it.

Her mother's shoulders eased, just slightly. "How are you feeling today?"

Idunnu shrugged, then decided to be honest. "Better. Nervous. But... better."

"That's allowed," her mother said.

Idunnu nodded and took another bite.

Her father entered the kitchen, adjusting his shirt cuffs as if he were preparing for work. He looked at Idunnu, and his face softened.

"My brilliant girl," he said, like it was a fact, not a compliment.

Idunnu's lips twitched. "Good morning."

He kissed the top of her head and sat for a moment, taking a sip of tea from his own mug.c"You have school today," he said.

"I know."

"And you will be fine," he added.

Idunnu didn't answer right away because fine was a word that had betrayed her before. But she could say something else. "I'm trying,"

Her father nodded, satisfied with that. "Trying is how you win battles."

Idunnu glanced toward the living room where her brother lay half-sprawled on the couch, pretending to read while actually listening.

He lifted his eyes and gave her a small grin. "Go and show them."

She rolled her eyes, but it didn't feel heavy. "Show them what?"

"That you're still you,"

Idunnu looked down at her plate. She took one more bite.

Then she stood, picked up her bag, and breathed out.

"Okay," she whispered. "I'm going."

Her School had a memory. The gates, the corridor, the smell of disinfectant and perfume and paper—everything carried echoes. But when Idunnu walked in, she didn't walk alone.

Mia spotted her first, her face brightening like someone had turned on a light.

"There she is!" Mia said, and hugged her carefully.

Zainab and Kemi followed, both smiling with relief.

"You look… stronger," Kemi said.

Idunnu exhaled. "I'm working on it."

Zainab adjusted the strap of her bag and studied Idunnu's face the way she always did, like she was reading between lines. "If you need to leave class, you tell me."

"I will."

They walked together, and for the first time in a long time, Idunnu felt the simple comfort of moving through school with people who didn't want anything from her except her presence.

In the hallway, she saw them.

Sienna and her friends. They didn't approach. They didn't smirk. They didn't perform. They just looked away. The space they gave her felt like a boundary the school had finally drawn in ink.

Idunnu didn't feel triumphant. She felt… safe.

English class was where things began to shift. Mr. Harris stood at the front of the room with a stack of papers and the kind of energy teachers got when they were about to announce something that would make students groan.

"Alright," he said, clapping his hands once. "Settle down. I've got an announcement."

The room quieted. Mr. Harris smiled. "The school's annual essay competition is open." A ripple moved through the class—whispers, raised brows, a few excited murmurs.

Idunnu's stomach tightened. Essay competition; she'd heard students talking about it in the corridors like it was a golden ticket.

Mr. Harris continued, "The prize is one thousand pounds."

That did it.

Someone whistled. Someone else muttered, "No way."

Mr. Harris held up a hand. "Yes, yes. One thousand. And the winning essay will also be published in the school's annual journal and two of the biggest newspapers in England!"

Idunnu felt Mia's elbow nudge her gently.

"You should do it," Mia whispered.

Idunnu didn't respond because the idea of putting her words in front of strangers made her chest tighten. She knew words were powerful. And power could attract attention.

Mr. Harris handed out the sheets. "Topic is open, but it must be true. A personal story. Something you've lived, something you've learned. I want honesty. I want voice."

Idunnu stared at the paper when it reached her desk.

*A personal story,* her hands went slightly cold.

That evening, she sat on the edge of her bed with a blank page in front of her. The radiator hummed softly. The house was quiet. Her pen hovered.

And her mind did what it always did when she tried to be brave. It listed reasons she shouldn't.

Other students were better. Other students weren't kidnapped. They didn't help find their brother. Other students didn't start their life from scratch. Other students hadn't fainted in class. Other students hadn't become the girl people whispered about.

Her phone buzzed.

A message from Mia: *Enter it. Please. Your words matter.*

Idunnu stared at the screen until it dimmed. Then she set the phone down as the blank page stared back. She could almost hear Sienna's voice from weeks ago—sweet and sharp.

"If you don't eat, you'll faint. And then everyone will really have something to talk about."

She didn't want to be something people talked about. She wanted to be someone people understood.

A knock came at her door.

Her father stepped in and looked at the blank page and the pen.

"Essay?" he asked.

Idunnu's shoulders slumped. "There's a competition."

"And you're entering."

She let out a short laugh that held no humor. "I don't know if I should."

Her father tilted his head. "Why not?"

Idunnu stared at the page. "Because there are so many good writers here."

"Idunnu," he said softly, "do you know who the best writer in the world is?"

She blinked. "Who?"

"You," he said.

She shook her head immediately. "Daddy, good writers who were born and raised here; who grew up speaking English, unlike me. They will be far better than me in writing."

"I'm not saying it because I'm your father," he interrupted, voice steady. "I'm saying it because I've watched you survive. I've watched you turn pain into words. That is not common."

Idunnu's eyes stung.

Her father continued, "Your story has power. And power is not something you hide because other people might be loud."

From the hallway, her mother's voice floated in. "Your father is right." Mrs. Adebayo appeared in the doorway, drying her hands on a towel. "Your story is yours alone," she said. "And you tell it beautifully."

Her brother's footsteps padded down the hall, and he leaned against the doorframe like he'd been there the whole time. "You should do it," he said. "Tell them about Nigeria. Tell them what we went through."

Idunnu's chest tightened. Her brother's eyes were serious. "If anyone can make them feel it, it's you."

Idunnu looked at her family. They weren't asking her to perform; they were asking her to speak. She turned back to the page as the pen touched down.

And the first sentence came out like a breath she'd been holding for years.

# Chapter 18:
# The Essay

She wrote over the next few days the way someone builds a bridge.

Carefully. One plank at a time. She began with Nigeria—not the fear, not yet, but the life. The markets with their bright fabrics and loud bargaining. The smell of fried plantain. The way neighbors called each other by name, the way laughter could travel across a street like music. She wrote about the parts of herself that had been formed there—her love for art, her habit of noticing details, her hunger for language.

Then she turned the page into the moment everything changed. She wrote about the day fear became a shadow that followed her. About the way danger can look ordinary until it isn't. About the moment she realized her brother was in trouble. About the way her hands shook when she drew—how she forced them to be steady anyway.

How she used lines and shapes to capture faces. How she listened, how she remembered, how she refused to let panic swallow her whole. She didn't write herself as a superhero. She wrote herself as a girl who was terrified. And who did what she had to do anyway.

When she finished, her hands were cramped and her eyes were swollen. But her chest felt lighter. Like she had taken something heavy out of her body and placed it on paper where it could no longer poison her silently.

**

On the day she handed it in, Idunnu expected her stomach to twist.

It didn't.

She walked to Mr. Harris's desk and placed the essay down. He looked up. "You entered?"

Idunnu nodded.

His expression softened. "Good." That was all he said.

But it was enough.

**

The assembly hall was packed. Students sat in neat rows, their whispers blending into a low hum that rose and fell like waves. Idunnu sat somewhere in the middle with Mia on one side and Zainab on the other. Kemi sat just behind them. Idunnu's fingers worried the edge of her sleeve.

"You okay?" Mia whispered.

Idunnu nodded tightly. "Just nervous."

"Even if you don't win," Mia said, "it's amazing you entered."

Idunnu tried to smile but her mind was a storm of hope and doubt.

The chatter quieted as the headmaster stepped onto the stage. He was tall and composed, holding a crisp white envelope.

"Good morning, students and staff," he began, voice echoing through the hall. "One of our proudest traditions is the annual essay competition."

He paused.

"This year, we received more entries than we ever have before. The judges were impressed by the quality of writing." The headmaster continued, "But one story stood out—not only for its craftsmanship, but for the power of its message."

Idunnu's palms went damp.

"It reminded us," he said, "that courage is not always loud. Sometimes it is quiet. Sometimes it is a girl who refuses to let fear have the final word."

Mia's hand found hers.

"The first-place prize," the headmaster said, "goes to…"

The pause felt endless.

"…Idunnu Adebayo."

For a second, the hall didn't make sense. The sound arrived late.

*Applause.*

*Cheers.*

Idunnu sat frozen, her brain refusing to accept what her ears had heard. Mia squeezed her hand hard. "That's you."

Zainab nudged her gently. "Go."

Idunnu stood on legs that felt like they belonged to someone else. The aisle stretched long as she walked, but with each step, something inside her steadied. She climbed the stairs to the stage. The headmaster smiled warmly as he handed her a certificate and a large ceremonial cheque with her name printed across it.

"Congratulations," he said. "Your story is extraordinary. It speaks of resilience. It speaks of courage. And it reminds us of the importance of sharing one's voice."

Idunnu's throat tightened as she looked out at the crowd. Faces turned toward her—some curious, some admiring, some softened by whatever her words had done to them. She didn't feel like a spectacle; she felt like a person.

The headmaster leaned in slightly. "We've also decided to publish your essay in the school's annual journal, and of course, newspapers too."

Idunnu blinked fast.

"Thank you," she whispered, voice barely audible over the applause.

After assembly, the corridor became a river of people. Students stopped her—some shy, some bold, all speaking at once.

"That was you?"

"I didn't know you could write like that."

"I cried."

"My mum would love that story."

Idunnu smiled until her cheeks ached. Not because she wanted attention, because for once, attention didn't feel like a weapon.

Mia hugged her first. "I'm proud of you," she said.

"You did it." Zainab nodded once, eyes bright.

Idunnu held the certificate carefully, like it might vanish. Mr. Harris caught her near the classroom door. "Idunnu," he said, voice low so it felt private, "It was beautiful. Your story made everyone realize that every chapter is important in life. I hope you realize how gifted you are."

Idunnu swallowed. "I just… wrote what happened."

"That's exactly it," he said. "This isn't just an essay. It's a beacon."

Idunnu looked down at the paper in her hands.

A beacon.

Something that helped people see.

**

That night, she sat at her desk at home. The certificate leaned against a stack of books. The ceremonial cheque was folded carefully and placed where her mother could not accidentally spill tea on it.

Idunnu stared at the blank page in her notebook.

Her father's words returned to her, quiet and steady, *'your words have power.'*

She thought about the girl she had been when she first arrived in the UK—hopeful, frightened, and trying to fit into a world that didn't know what she carried. She thought about the girl she had been in the hospital bed—small, exhausted, finally telling the truth.

And she thought about the girl she was now.

Not unstoppable, not invincible, but standing. She picked up her pen. This time, she didn't write for prize money. She wrote because she had found her voice.

And she intended to use it.

# Chapter 20:
# The Recovery

The morning light slipped through the curtains and turned Idunnu's desk into something almost holy—golden edges on paper, soft warmth on the wood, a quiet invitation. She sat with her pen poised above a fresh sheet, smiling to herself as if the words were already there and she only had to catch them.

It had been months since the essay competition. Months since her hands had trembled as she walked up to the stage. Months since her story—*Every Lesson Counts*—had become more than an assignment.

The ripples still moved. At school, she had become a name people said with a different kind of tone. Not the tone of gossip and not the tone of cruelty, but something softer. Something like respect.

In the corridors, teachers stopped her to ask how she was doing. Students who had never spoken to her before offered shy smiles, or quick, awkward congratulations. Some asked questions—careful ones, as if they were afraid of touching a bruise.

And her teachers—especially the ones who had once marked her work with red ink and firm comments—looked at her now with pride that didn't feel performative.

Her Fine Art teacher had held up one of Idunnu's sketches after class and said, "You see? Your eyes have always known how to tell the truth."

Her French teacher had smiled when Idunnu answered a question without hesitation and said, "*Très bien.* Your voice is stronger than you think."

Some students had even given her a nickname.

*The artist. The linguist. The detective.*

At first, it embarrassed her. Then, slowly, she understood what it really meant. They weren't calling her perfect. They were calling her proof. Proof that a girl could be broken and still become whole again. Proof that learning wasn't just for exams.

Proof that survival could be stitched together from small skills—drawn lines, remembered words, the courage to pay attention.

That was why she had decided to write the letter; for the people who had taught her without knowing what they were preparing her for.

She pulled a clean page from her notebook and began.

*"Dear Teachers,*

*I never imagined the day would arrive when I would be writing a letter like this. If I'm honest, I was not the best student. I didn't excel in every subject. I wasn't the one who always raised my hand first. Sometimes I was the one who asked, "When am I ever going to use this?" or "How will this help me in real life?"*

*Now I know the answer. Months ago, my brother and I were abducted back in Nigeria. It was the most frightening experience of my life. In the darkness, though, I found strength in places I didn't expect.*

*When the authorities were trying to identify the men who took us, one of the strongest tools we had come from what I learned in Fine Art. I sketched faces—details I had trained myself to notice without even realizing it.*

*And when I heard the kidnappers speaking French, it was vocabulary lessons I had only half-listened to that helped me understand something important.*

*I used what you taught me to help save my brother. I understand now that your patience and persistence mattered more than I ever knew.*

*Thank you for teaching me even when I didn't appreciate it. Thank you for pushing me even when I complained. Thank you for giving me skills that became more than schoolwork.*

*Because of you, learning is no longer a chore to me.*

*It is a gift.*

*With gratitude,*

*Idunnu Adebayo.*

When she finished, Idunnu sat back and stared at the page.

Her handwriting looked steadier than it used to. She folded the letter carefully, as if she were folding something fragile and precious, and slid it into an envelope. She addressed it to her Fine Art teacher and her French teacher, knowing they would share it with the staff.

As she tucked it into her schoolbag, a wave of peace moved through her—quiet, deep, and surprising. It wasn't the loud kind of happiness.

It was the kind that settled.

She glanced around her room. Her sketches were pinned neatly on the wall now, no longer just assignments but evidence—proof of her eye, her patience, her courage. Her French workbook sat open on her desk, the pages filled with notes and underlines, no longer a source of frustration but a bridge to the moment she had needed it most.

Downstairs, her mother called her name.

Idunnu answered, "Coming!"

**

The next day at school, the whispers followed her again, but they weren't sharp. They were full of awe—the kind that made her uncomfortable, but also grateful.

In the art room, she watched students who used to avoid drawing now experimenting with charcoal and paint. Someone had even asked her how she shaded faces so realistically.

In French class, the usual groans were replaced by laughter and curiosity. A boy near the front raised his hand.

"Madame," he asked, "how do you say 'hero' in French?"

The teacher's eyes flicked to Idunnu for a second—warm, proud.

"*Héros,*" she answered.

The boy nodded seriously. "Because that's what Idunnu is."

The class erupted—not in mockery, not in cruelty—just a burst of applause and laughter, the kind that made Idunnu's cheeks burn. She lowered her eyes, smiling despite herself. Not because she wanted to be called a hero, but because she finally understood something important.

That evening, the sun set over Stoke-on-Trent in slow, pink streaks. At her desk, Idunnu opened a new notebook.

No competition. No judges. No prize money.

Just *her*.

She wrote the title at the top of the first page, carefully, as if naming something gave it shape.

*Every Lesson Counts.*

Then she paused. She thought of Nigeria—of markets and laughter. She thought of fear—how it had tried to swallow her. She thought of London—how it had tested her. She thought of her family—how they had held her up when she couldn't hold herself.

And she thought of the girl she used to be, the one who believed she had to be silent to survive. Idunnu placed her pen to the paper. This time, she didn't write to prove anything. She wrote to make meaning. To turn pain into purpose. To leave a light behind for the version of herself who once thought she would never feel whole again.

Outside, the sky deepened into twilight. Inside, Idunnu's words began to move. And for the first time in a long time, the future didn't feel like a threat.

It felt like a page.

www.ingramcontent.com/pod-product-compliance
Lightning Source LLC
Chambersburg PA
CBHW051543050726
47595CB00002B/612